THE PREQUEL TRILOGY STORIES

Based on the story and screenplay by
George Lucas

Illustrations by
Brian Rood

LUCASFILM
PRESS

LOS ANGELES • NEW YORK

© & TM 2017 Lucasfilm Ltd.

All rights reserved. Published by Disney • Lucasfilm Press, an imprint of Disney Book Group. No part of this book may be reproduced or transmitted in any form or by any means, electronic or mechanical, including photocopying, recording, or by any information storage and retrieval system, without written permission from the publisher. For information address Disney Press, 1101 Flower Street, Glendale, California 91201.

"Short Negotiations" written by Andy Schmidt
"Escaping Naboo" written by Rebecca L. Schmidt
"The Path of a Podracer" written by S.T. Bende
"A Different Path" written by Elizabeth Schaefer
"Droid Attack!" written by Meredith Rusu
"The Final Fight" written by Ivan Cohen
"Ambushed!" written by Andy Schmidt
"The Secret Army" written by Meredith Rusu
"Anakin's Vow" written by Elizabeth Schaefer
"A Deadly Plot" written by Meredith Rusu
"Into the Arena" written by Ivan Cohen
"The Brink of War" written by Rebecca L. Schmidt
"The Duel with Dooku" written by Ivan Cohen
"The Cyborg and the Jedi" written by Elizabeth Schaefer
"Driven to the Dark Side" written by S.T. Bende
"Empire Ascendant" written by Andy Schmidt
"The Rule of Two" written by Rebecca L. Schmidt
"Darth Vader Rises" written by Rebecca L. Schmidt

Printed in the United States of America

First Edition, September 2017

1 3 5 7 9 10 8 6 4 2

FAC-038091-17223

Library of Congress Control Number on file

ISBN 978-1-4847-5907-3

Visit the official *Star Wars* website at: www.starwars.com

THE STAR WARS SAGA

TIMELINE

 THE PHANTOM MENACE

 ATTACK OF THE CLONES

 REVENGE OF THE SITH

 A NEW HOPE

 THE EMPIRE STRIKES BACK

 RETURN OF THE JEDI

 THE FORCE AWAKENS

CHARACTERS

ANAKIN SKYWALKER/ DARTH VADER
THE CHOSEN ONE

OBI-WAN KENOBI
BRAVE JEDI MASTER

QUI-GON JINN
LEGENDARY JEDI MASTER

PADMÉ AMIDALA
QUEEN AND SENATOR OF NABOO

DARTH MAUL
SITH APPRENTICE

JAR JAR BINKS
FRIEND OF THE GALACTIC REPUBLIC

YODA
OLD AND WISE JEDI MASTER

MACE WINDU
FORMIDABLE JEDI MASTER

JANGO FETT
BOUNTY HUNTER

GENERAL GRIEVOUS
SUPREME COMMANDER OF
THE DROID ARMY

COUNT DOOKU
FALLEN JEDI AND
SEPARATIST LEADER

**SENATOR PALPATINE/
DARTH SIDIOUS**
SUPREME CHANCELLOR OF
THE GALACTIC REPUBLIC
AND SITH LORD

CONTENTS

THE PHANTOM MENACE

Short Negotiations 1

Escaping Naboo 15

The Path of a Podracer 31

A Different Path 49

Droid Attack! 65

The Final Fight 81

ATTACK OF THE CLONES

Ambushed! 97

The Secret Army 111

Anakin's Vow 127

A Deadly Plot 143

Into the Arena 159

The Brink of War 175

Revenge of the Sith

The Duel with Dooku 195

The Cyborg and the Jedi 211

Driven to the Dark Side 227

Empire Ascendant 243

The Rule of Two 261

Darth Vader Rises 277

A long time ago in a galaxy far, far away. . . .

SHORT NEGOTIATIONS

SHORT NEGOTIATIONS

Jedi Master Qui-Gon Jinn and his Jedi apprentice, Obi-Wan Kenobi, flew in their star cruiser toward the planet of Naboo. The notorious Trade Federation had created a web of space stations around the planet that prevented anyone from coming or going. This blockade also meant that the people of Naboo were not getting the supplies they desperately needed. The Jedi had been sent by the Supreme Chancellor of the galaxy-spanning Republic. It was up to Qui-Gon and Obi-Wan to convince the Trade Federation to remove the blockade once and for all.

When they arrived at the blockade base, Qui-Gon and Obi-Wan were greeted by a silver protocol droid.

"We are greatly honored by your visit, ambassadors," said the droid.

However, despite the droid's kind words, it would soon become clear that the Trade Federation was not going to meet with them at all.

"I have a bad feeling about this," Obi-Wan said.

Qui-Gon was not concerned.

"These Federation types are cowards. The negotiations will be short."

Meanwhile, aboard the bridge of the blockade station, Viceroy Nute Gunray was already panicking.

The viceroy contacted Darth Sidious, an evil and powerful Sith Lord who was secretly in charge of the Trade Federation. Even as a hologram, Darth Sidious was a terrifying presence.

"This scheme of yours has failed, Lord Sidious," the viceroy's second-in-command pleaded. "The blockade is finished! We dare not go against these Jedi."

But Darth Sidious would not listen.

"Kill them immediately!" ordered the Sith Lord.

Short Negotiations

The viceroy acted quickly, ordering that the Jedi's Republic Cruiser be destroyed! The visitors would have no way to escape from the blockade!

Qui-Gon and Obi-Wan were still waiting for the viceroy in a separate room on board the base.

"I sense an unusual amount of fear for something as trivial as this trade dispute," said Qui-Gon.

Just then, the blast doors locked in place. The Jedi ignited their lightsabers in a flash, but toxic gas began to fill the air! Qui-Gon and Obi-Wan were trapped!

STAR WARS STORYBOOK COLLECTION

After a few minutes, the viceroy ordered his battle droids to capture the Jedi.

"They must be unconscious by now," he said.

When the doors opened, the battle droids cautiously entered the cloudy room, only to be met by Obi-Wan and Qui-Gon! The Jedi were alive and well.

Short Negotiations

"Blast them!" ordered the lead droid.

But the battle droids were no match for the two Jedi. Qui-Gon dismantled robotic soldiers left and right while Obi-Wan used the Force to push a group of them through the air and smash them onto the ground!

With the battle droids defeated, Qui-Gon sensed the viceroy through a heavy blast door and plunged his lightsaber through the barrier.

The viceroy was shocked to see his soldiers defeated so easily. "Send in the droidekas," he commanded.

Short Negotiations

As the even deadlier destroyer droids started firing, Obi-Wan began blocking the blasts with his lightsaber! But the fiery bolts were coming too quickly and the droidekas had shield generators to protect them.

Qui-Gon realized they wouldn't have enough time to get through the door.

"It's a standoff! Let's go!"

Qui-Gon and Obi-Wan slipped away and managed to find the large hangar bays on the base. There they saw thousands of battle droids being loaded onto massive carrier ships that were headed to the planet's surface.

"It's an invasion army," Obi-Wan said.

"This is an odd play for the Trade Federation," said Qui-Gon.

The two Jedi hid on board the carrier ships. They needed to inform the Supreme Chancellor, but more important, they had to find a way to warn the people of Naboo!

ESCAPING NABOO

ESCAPING NABOO

Qui-Gon Jinn glanced up at the skies as he crashed through the forests of Naboo. He and his Jedi apprentice, Obi-Wan Kenobi, had narrowly escaped from the evil Trade Federation's clutches. Now the Jedi Knight was powerless as he watched battleships full of droid soldiers land on the innocent planet.

Qui-Gon and Obi-Wan needed to warn the people of Naboo before the Trade Federation took over.

STAR WARS STORYBOOK COLLECTION

The Jedi didn't get very far before they saw a tall alien about to be run over by a giant tank! Qui-Gon saved the stranger just in time. But when the Jedi tried to send the alien away, he refused!

"No . . . no! Mesa stay. . . . Mesa called Jar Jar Binks. Mesa your humble servant," the alien replied.

Jar Jar told the Jedi about a safe underwater city where his people, the Gungans, lived.

Qui-Gon needed help. This hidden city sounded like a good start. But when Qui-Gon told Jar Jar to lead the way, Jar Jar was suddenly scared. He had been banished from Otoh Gunga and could never return.

Qui-Gon and Obi-Wan wouldn't take no for an answer, and soon the unlikely trio was swimming deep, deep, deep into a large lake until they arrived at the mysterious underwater city.

The Jedi were brought before the city's leader, Boss Nass.

Qui-Gon hoped that the Gungan leader would aid them in warning the Naboo, but Boss Nass believed his people were well hidden from the Trade Federation.

"Wesa no care-n about da Naboo," Boss Nass told Qui-Gon.

The Jedi had no choice but to continue on their mission without the Gungans' help. However, they were given transport through the planet's core, as well as a guide—Jar Jar!

Obi-Wan piloted the companions through the dark waters of the planet's core. He could barely see in front of him. Suddenly, there was a great *crunch*! A monstrous fish was trying to take a bite out of their submarine!

"Big gooberfish! Huge-o teeth!" shouted Jar Jar.

Obi-Wan wrestled the ship free, but the gooberfish's bite had damaged the vessel. It soon lost power.

Luckily, Obi-Wan had been trained well by Qui-Gon, and the Padawan quickly got the ship back up and running again, only to reveal another monstrous fish! This one was even bigger than the last one. Jar Jar yelped in panic, but Obi-Wan deftly piloted the ship away from the monster's jaws and into an outcropping. They were finally out of danger.

The Jedi soon reached the planet's surface, but they were too late. Not only had the Trade Federation beaten them to Naboo's capital city, but it had captured the planet's leader, Queen Amidala. The Jedi needed to rescue her!

Qui-Gon led Obi-Wan and Jar Jar into the city. They snuck through the streets, avoiding droid patrols until they found the queen, her security forces, and her handmaidens being led away by Trade Federation troops.

Obi-Wan and Qui-Gon leapt over a balcony and, with a few brief slashes of their lightsabers, took down the troops.

"We should leave the streets," Qui-Gon said, leading the group toward a hangar.

Now that they had Queen Amidala, Qui-Gon realized they had to get her off Naboo. Queen Amidala didn't want to leave her people, but Qui-Gon convinced her that only under the protection of the Galactic Senate and the Supreme Chancellor on Coruscant could she begin the battle to win back her planet.

The hangar was full of droid troops that stopped Qui-Gon and the others as soon as they reached the queen's ship.

ESCAPING NABOO

"I'm ambassador for the Supreme Chancellor, and I'm taking these people to Coruscant," Qui-Gon said.

"That doesn't compute," the droid commander replied. "You're under arrest!"

Resorting to more aggressive negotiations, Qui-Gon and Obi-Wan used their lightsabers to silence the droid soldiers so the queen and her entourage could board the ship.

The queen's ship rocketed away from the hangar, but Qui-Gon and his companions weren't free yet. They needed to get past the Trade Federation's blockade of ships surrounding the planet. They were just one ship, and they didn't have a lot of weapons. They would have to make a run for it.

Suddenly, the ship jolted. They had been hit—badly.

"The shield generator's out!" shouted the captain.

Qui-Gon was worried. Without the shields, they wouldn't last long against the blockade. They had to send out droids to fix the shield generator.

ESCAPING NABOO

The ship's company of droids, including a small blue-and-white R2 unit, quickly began repairs. But the Trade Federation wasn't going to give up without a fight. It aimed its weapons at the droids!

"We're losing droids fast," Obi-Wan said.

Soon only the small R2 unit was left. Would he be able to fix the ship on his own?

With a buzz, the shields came back to life!

The droid had done it! With the shields back on, the ship safely made it past the blockade and into hyperspace.

Qui-Gon met with Queen Amidala as she commended the droid that had saved them. "What is its number?" she asked her security officer.

"Artoo-Detoo," he replied.

"Thank you, Artoo-Detoo," the queen said, smiling at the small droid.

The ship was still badly damaged. They would need to land on a nearby planet to make repairs. But Qui-Gon and Obi-Wan had rescued the queen and escaped Naboo, and that was a good start.

THE PATH OF A PODRACER

The Path of a Podracer

Jedi Knight Qui-Gon Jinn was in trouble. He and his Padawan, Obi-Wan Kenobi, may have rescued Queen Amidala, but they had failed to convince the Trade Federation to lift the blockade surrounding Naboo. The Jedi needed to take the queen to Coruscant so she could urge the Senate to help her people, but the ship they were traveling in was badly damaged. Qui-Gon, Obi-Wan, the queen, and her attendants were forced to make an emergency landing on an Outer Rim planet called Tatooine. Settlements on the desert planet were scarce, and Qui-Gon had little time to find supplies and fix their transport. Without the right parts, they'd never make it to Coruscant . . . and the citizens of Naboo would continue to suffer.

Before Qui-Gon set off to locate the supplies they needed, the queen insisted one of her handmaidens, Padmé, join him. Qui-Gon led Padmé, Jar Jar Binks, and R2-D2 across the desert and into a cramped junk shop, where a winged creature named Watto hovered behind the counter.

"Watch the store!" Watto barked at a young slave boy named Anakin before turning to help Qui-Gon.

Watto had what Qui-Gon needed, but he wouldn't accept the Jedi's Republic credits. The group left the junk shop empty-handed. If they couldn't find another way to pay Watto, they wouldn't make it to Coruscant.

Fierce winds whipped sand across the desert. A storm was quickly approaching.

The boy from the shop invited Qui-Gon, Jar Jar, Padmé, and R2-D2 to take shelter with him, so the group followed Anakin home.

Anakin introduced everyone to his mother, Shmi. The boy was happy to have new friends in his home, but he was particularly fond of Padmé.

"I built a protocol droid to help Mom. Come on, I'll show you Threepio!"

The unfinished droid blinked to life.

"Hello, I am See-Threepio, human-cyborg relations." C-3PO tottered over to the small blue-and-white droid, who beeped a loud greeting. "Artoo-Detoo, a pleasure to meet you."

STAR WARS STORYBOOK COLLECTION

Over dinner, Qui-Gon explained that they were traveling to Coruscant and needed supplies to repair their ship.

Anakin knew what to do.

"There's a big race tomorrow on Boonta Eve. You could enter my pod. The prize money would more than pay for the parts."

Podracers flew fast ships through narrow canyons. Anakin's mother was afraid for her son. But Shmi agreed that he should enter on Qui-Gon's behalf.

"He was meant to help you."

Qui-Gon sensed the Force was strong with Anakin. He wanted to train the boy to become a Jedi. When the storm passed, Qui-Gon approached Watto with a wager. Watto agreed to let Anakin race but refused to trade Anakin's podracer for the family's freedom.

After some discussion, the two decided that Anakin could earn his freedom by beating an alien named Sebulba—but Anakin's mother would remain a slave.

STAR WARS STORYBOOK COLLECTION

Cheering spectators filled the stands on the day of the race. As the announcers introduced the racers, Sebulba secretly loosened a piece of Anakin's podracer.

"Use your instincts." Qui-Gon adjusted Anakin's helmet. "May the Force be with you."

A wealthy gangster named Jabba the Hutt sounded the gong, and the roar of the crowd echoed across the desert. Dust billowed in

THE PATH OF A PODRACER

enormous clouds and engines growled loudly as the racers burst from the starting line to careen around the first corner.

But Anakin's podracer stalled. He couldn't move!

Anakin flipped switches and shuffled cords, reengineering his podracer until it surged forward. Anakin had to make up for lost time!

Tusken Raiders lurked in the dunes, firing blasts that sent racers off course. But Anakin flew with exceptional skill, darting through rocky arches and around the wreckage of unlucky podracers.

Anakin started his final lap directly behind Sebulba. But the piece of the boy's podracer that the alien had tampered with earlier suddenly flew off, and Anakin's podracer started to stream black smoke!

As Anakin struggled to balance his engines, Sebulba slammed into him. But the alien's dirty trick backfired. The attack made Sebulba's engine explode! The alien crashed hard in the dry sand. Sebulba was out of the race!

Anakin kept a tight grip on his podracer and sped through the finish line to take first place. The crowd burst into cheers!

"Mom, I did it!" Anakin cried as Qui-Gon lifted him onto his shoulders.

"You have brought hope to those who have none." Shmi smiled. "I'm so very proud of you."

Qui-Gon used the prize money to buy the supplies they needed and gave Shmi the money he earned selling the podracer. Then he told the Skywalkers about his wager: Anakin's win had earned the boy his freedom and the chance to train as a Jedi.

Shmi hugged her son. "Now you can make your dreams come true."

"What about Mom?" Anakin asked Qui-Gon. "Is she free, too?"

Qui-Gon frowned.

"I tried to free your mother, too, but Watto wouldn't let me."

Anakin was excited to train as a Jedi, but he didn't want to leave his mother. He wondered if he would ever see her again.

"What does your heart tell you?" she asked.

"I will come back and free you, Mom," Anakin said. "I promise."

Shmi cupped Anakin's face tenderly.

"We'll see each other again."

Then she squeezed his shoulders and turned him toward Qui-Gon. With his mother's encouragement, Anakin took his first brave steps on his path to becoming a Jedi.

A hover bike raced toward Anakin and Qui-Gon as they neared their ship. A cloaked creature with a red-and-black face flipped over the bike, activated a lightsaber, and launched himself at Qui-Gon.

Anakin scrambled onto the starship as Qui-Gon began to duel the mysterious opponent.

The hum of clashing weapons echoed across the desert as the creature's powerful strokes drove Qui-Gon backward. The Jedi's lightsaber shook as he blocked the intruder's blows. Qui-Gon couldn't hold him off much longer!

Just as the creature jumped into the air to strike Qui-Gon down, the Jedi leapt onto the lowered ramp of the ship. The doors closed and the starship flew away. Qui-Gon had escaped!

STAR WARS STORYBOOK COLLECTION

On board the ship and puzzled by what had just happened, Qui-Gon distracted himself by introducing Anakin to Obi-Wan.

"You're a Jedi, too?" Anakin asked as he shook Obi-Wan's hand. "Pleased to meet you!"

Qui-Gon knew that the Force had brought the three of them together. He had gone to Tatooine looking for supplies, but what he had found was far more valuable—and may have even had the power to change the balance of the Force forever.

A DIFFERENT PATH

A Different Path

Anakin Skywalker looked through the viewport of Queen Amidala's cruiser and saw an amazing sight—the planet of Coruscant.

Over the centuries, Coruscant's many large cities had grown so big that they finally became one city that stretched across the entire planet.

The billions of twinkling lights below made Anakin feel very small. He had just left his home planet of Tatooine for the first time. Although he was happy to be with his new friends—especially the queen's handmaiden, Padmé—he was nervous about his future. . . .

The Jedi Knight Qui-Gon Jinn had taken Anakin to Coruscant to present the boy to the Jedi Council. Qui-Gon believed that Anakin was strong in the Force and destined to become a Jedi Knight himself. Perhaps Anakin could even help the Jedi track down the mysterious stranger who had attacked them before they left Tatooine. But first Qui-Gon needed the Council's permission to train Anakin.

The Council worried that Anakin was too old to begin training, but Qui-Gon pleaded with them. "I request the boy be tested," he said.

Master Yoda and Mace Windu exchanged looks. Then Mace finally said, "Bring him before us, then."

While Anakin was fighting for the chance to become a Jedi, Queen Amidala was fighting to save her people. Even though the Trade Federation was attacking her home planet of Naboo, the Galactic Senate refused to help her. The Senate didn't want to believe that something so terrible was happening.

Amidala refused to be ignored. With the support of her friend Senator Palpatine, the queen suggested that the Senate elect a new leader—one who would not overlook the suffering of Naboo and other worlds.

When Anakin was brought before the Council, the Jedi asked him many questions. But no question troubled Anakin as much as Master Yoda's.

"Afraid are you?" Yoda asked.

Anakin thought of his mother, left behind on Tatooine. He thought of how afraid he was to lose her. If he didn't become a Jedi, her sacrifice would have been for nothing.

All those thoughts swirled through Anakin's mind as Yoda spoke: "Fear is the path to the dark side. Fear leads to anger. Anger leads to hate. Hate leads to suffering."

Yoda paused and looked directly at Anakin. "I sense much fear in you."

STAR WARS STORYBOOK COLLECTION

Amidala paced in Senator Palpatine's office. The Senate had taken her advice and voted to replace the current leader with none other than Senator Palpatine himself!

A Different Path

With Senator Palpatine advocating for her cause in the Senate, the queen decided to return to her home planet of Naboo and do what she could to help the situation on the ground.

After Anakin's test, the Council met with Qui-Gon.

"The Force is strong with him," one Jedi started.

"He is to be trained, then?" Qui-Gon asked.

"No," Mace finished.

Qui-Gon couldn't believe the Jedi would turn away such a promising student. He demanded an explanation.

"Clouded, the boy's future is," Yoda told Qui-Gon. "Young Skywalker's fate will be decided later."

With the Senate choosing a new leader and Amidala confronting the Trade Federation, much about the future was uncertain. Yoda instructed Qui-Gon to go with Queen Amidala back to Naboo.

Anakin was worried that the Jedi had not accepted him. But Qui-Gon was determined to teach Anakin one way or another. Before they reached Naboo, he told Anakin, "I'm not allowed to train you, so I want you to watch me and be mindful."

Anakin resolved to learn everything he could from Qui-Gon and everyone else around him. If that was going to be his first and last mission, he wanted to make it count.

When they landed on Naboo, Amidala revealed her plan. She knew they had no chance of defeating the Trade Federation by themselves. But although the humans on Naboo had been imprisoned, the water-dwelling Gungans below the planet's surface were still free.

Anakin watched as the queen made her plea before the Gungans' leader, Boss Nass.

"We wish to form an alliance," she began. She looked uncertain—an expression Anakin wasn't used to seeing on the queen's face.

Suddenly, Padmé stepped forward and interrupted. "I am Queen Amidala."

The queen explained that she had disguised herself as a handmaiden for protection.

Anakin was shocked! He realized the brave girl he had befriended on Tatooine was actually the queen!

"Your Honor, our two great societies have always lived in peace," Queen Amidala said. "The Trade Federation has destroyed all that we have worked so hard to build."

The queen fell to her knees.

"I beg you to help us."

Boss Nass stroked his chin, making Amidala wait for his answer. Finally, he burst into laughter.

"Mesa lika dis. Maybe wesa bein friends."

But the leaders of the Trade Federation knew what Padmé was up to. The Sith Master, Darth Sidious, and his apprentice Darth Maul, the mysterious foe who had attacked Qui-Gon on Tatooine, had discovered the queen's growing army.

"She is more foolish than I thought," said Darth Sidious. "Wipe them out. All of them."

Anakin and Padmé would soon be facing their greatest challenges yet.

DROID ATTACK!

DROID ATTACK!

An army of Gungans waited nervously on the battlefield. Their home world, Naboo, was under attack! The evil Trade Federation had invaded the planet.

Luckily, the inhabitants of Naboo had a plan. The Gungans would hold off the Trade Federation's droid army while Naboo's starship pilots tried to blow up the space station controlling the robots. Meanwhile, Naboo's Queen Amidala and her soldiers would storm the palace and capture the Trade Federation viceroy. Only then would peace be restored.

"Starting up the shield," announced Gungan general Tobler Ceel.

A powerful energy force field lowered around the army like a protective bubble.

Ruuuuuumble. The ground shook as the droid army marched forward. There were so many of them! The Gungans were *really* nervous.

"Open fire!" ordered one of the droids.

ZAP! ZAP! ZAP!

The droids fired their laser guns. But the shield protected the Gungans.

They were safe . . . for now.

Meanwhile, Padmé and her soldiers stormed Naboo's royal palace, where the viceroy was hiding. Battle droids blocked their path.

"We don't have time for this," Padmé said to her guard, Captain Panaka. They needed to get to the throne room and capture the viceroy before the droid army became too much for the Gungans to hold off.

Captain Panaka had an idea. He used his blaster to shoot out a nearby window.

DROID ATTACK!

"Ascension guns!" he cried.

"Good thinking!" exclaimed Padmé.

The soldiers could use their ascension guns to shoot grappling hooks to the next window ledge and rise up to the throne room . . . from the outside!

"Go!" yelled Captain Panaka.

The group quickly did as he said. They were almost there!

Back on the battlefield, the droids unexpectedly ceased fire.

That couldn't be good. The Gungans shifted nervously.

"Steady, steady," Jar Jar Binks ordered his troops.

Enormous doors on the droid tanks suddenly opened. Racks holding thousands—no, tens of thousands!—of additional droid troops rolled out.

The Gungans gasped.

"Ouch time," General Ceel said to Jar Jar.

The massive droid army marched forward . . . and passed straight through the energy shield! Their tanks powered through, too.

STAR WARS STORYBOOK COLLECTION

"Fire!" yelled General Ceel.

The Gungans used all their weapons to battle the droids. But there were just too many. Jar Jar's troops cried out and scattered left and right to avoid the blaster fire.

"Retreat! Retreat!" yelled Jar Jar.

Back in Naboo's starship hangar, Anakin Skywalker hid in the cockpit of a starship. Jedi Master Qui-Gon Jinn had made Anakin promise to stay there so the boy would be safe during the battle.

But Anakin accidently turned on the ship's autopilot. Before he knew what was happening, the ship flew into the sky . . . and straight toward the battle between Naboo's starship pilots and the Trade Federation space station!

Even though he was young, Anakin was brave. He wanted to help!

With backup from his droid copilot, R2-D2, Anakin whizzed his ship left. He zipped it right. He did a barrel roll . . . right into a laser blast!

"We're hit, Artoo!" cried Anakin.

The boy's starship spiraled out of control and tumbled straight through the open doors of the space station's main hull.

Anakin desperately tried to get his ship up and running. He hit every button he could think of.

Pow! Pow! Without realizing it, Anakin shot two torpedoes straight at the space station's main reactor.

FZZZZZZT! The main reactor exploded!

"Let's get out of here!" Anakin yelled.

Anakin and R2-D2 escaped just in time.

The space station blew up from the inside!

"Woo-hoo!" cheered the other starship pilots. "Great job, Anakin!"

Below on the battlefield, the droid army stopped working!

"Whatsa they doing?" asked Jar Jar.

"The control ship has been destroyed!" said General Ceel. "Look!"

He pushed over a deactivated droid soldier. It tumbled to the ground harmlessly.

"Hooray!" cheered all the Gungans.

Anakin had destroyed the space station, and Padmé and her soldiers had successfully captured the viceroy, too. The droid army was defeated.

Naboo was free once again!

THE FINAL FIGHT

THE FINAL FIGHT

Jedi Knight Qui-Gon Jinn and his apprentice, Obi-Wan Kenobi, had arrived on Naboo alongside Queen Amidala with one goal: to capture Viceroy Nute Gunray, whose battle droids had taken control of the planet.

But as they headed toward the throne room, Qui-Gon saw Darth Maul—the mysterious Sith Lord he had battled on Tatooine—blocking their path.

Qui-Gon and Obi-Wan stepped forward to face Maul.

As the Jedi charged Darth Maul, the Sith Lord demonstrated incredible acrobatic skill, flipping through the air and wielding his double-bladed lightsaber to block Qui-Gon's and Obi-Wan's every move.

Maul was able to steer the Jedi into an adjoining room that contained a pit for the building's main power generator.

Lightsaber flashing, Darth Maul leapt onto a bridge high above, with Obi-Wan and Qui-Gon following close behind.

Qui-Gon chased Maul, navigating a series of energy barriers that would destroy anyone who got caught in them. Realizing that the barriers cycled on and off in a set pattern, Qui-Gon and Darth Maul painstakingly made their way forward to the generator's deadly melting pit, just a few barriers separating them from each other. Obi-Wan followed close behind but still had several barriers between him and his mentor.

When Qui-Gon finally reached Maul, the young Jedi watched helplessly as his mentor faced Darth Maul alone. Qui-Gon fought ferociously, ducking and parrying his enemy's attacks with dizzying speed!

But as Obi-Wan made it to the edge of the final energy barrier between him and his ally, the battle took an ugly turn. Darth Maul caught Qui-Gon off guard and landed a deadly blow.

Obi-Wan screamed as Qui-Gon collapsed to the floor.

When the energy gate cycled open, Obi-Wan charged at Maul, resuming the battle with a newfound ferocity.

Darth Maul attacked the young warrior relentlessly, using his mastery of the dark side of the Force to fling objects through the air, ultimately distracting Obi-Wan and sending him flying into the melting pit!

As Obi-Wan struggled to maintain a grip on the wall of the pit, Darth Maul kicked the Jedi's lightsaber into the seemingly bottomless depths.

Obi-Wan concentrated as Qui-Gon had taught him, reaching out with the Force even as Darth Maul drew closer. As the Sith Lord prepared to end Obi-Wan's life, the apprentice Jedi Knight soared out of the pit, summoning Qui-Gon's lightsaber to his hand along the way.

Wielding the lightsaber with deadly precision, he struck Darth Maul, sending the villain into the pit to his doom.

The Final Fight

Obi-Wan rushed to Qui-Gon's side, reaching his mentor just in time to hear his final wish. Qui-Gon urged his apprentice to train Anakin Skywalker, the young prodigy who Qui-Gon hoped would bring balance to the Force.

"Obi-Wan . . ." urged Qui-Gon, "promise me you'll train the boy."

"Yes, Master," agreed Obi-Wan, choking back tears as Qui-Gon breathed his last.

Hours later, a mournful Obi-Wan—reunited with Anakin Skywalker—watched as Supreme Chancellor Palpatine's cruiser landed in the courtyard outside the main hangar.

The Chancellor, accompanied by his guards, approached the pair.

"We are indebted to you for your bravery, Obi-Wan Kenobi," said Palpatine, adding, "and you, young Skywalker. We will watch your career with great interest."

But it was Obi-Wan's career that was to be confirmed that day.

"Confer on you the level of Jedi Knight, the Council does," said Jedi Master Yoda. "But agree with your taking this boy as your Padawan learner, I do not. Grave danger I fear."

But Obi-Wan remembered his promise to his Jedi Master.

"Qui-Gon believed in him, and I will train him. Without the approval of the Council, if I must."

Reluctantly, the wise old Yoda agreed.

"Your apprentice, young Skywalker will be."

At sunset, the central plaza of Naboo's capital city was filled with people who had gathered to honor Qui-Gon at the Jedi Knight's funeral.

Nearby, Yoda and Jedi Master Mace Windu discussed their suspicions about the true nature of the threat facing the Jedi.

"There is no doubt. Darth Maul was a Sith," said Mace.

Yoda considered this, adding, "Always two there are . . . a master . . . and an apprentice."

As the funeral came to an end, a worried Mace asked the question they would need to answer soon: "But which was destroyed, the master or the apprentice?"

STAR WARS STORYBOOK COLLECTION

As the Jedi Masters wondered if the battle with the Sith was truly over, there was still reason to celebrate. Naboo was free from the evil Trade Federation!

The crowds cheered their heroes, who were assembled on the giant staircase. Padmé and Anakin smiled at each other, happy to be together once more.

Whatever the future held, for then at least, the forces of good stood triumphant.

AMBUSHED!

Ambushed!

Padmé Amidala, the former queen of Naboo, flew toward the bustling planet of Coruscant. She was on her way to the Galactic Senate to represent her people once more as a senator.

Many people in the galaxy were unhappy with the Senate. Some, known as the Separatists, even used violence to show how angry they were.

The Jedi Knights were having difficulty maintaining peace throughout the galaxy. Padmé hoped that the Senate could help.

But when the senator's ship landed on the giant platform, there was a sudden explosion! Someone had laid a trap for Padmé!

Only the pilots of the two starfighters that had escorted the senator's ship escaped the fiery blast.

"M'lady, you are still in danger!" one pilot said to the other.

The other pilot removed her helmet, revealing that she was actually the senator in disguise!

Nearby, in Chancellor Palpatine's chambers, Jedi Council members Mace Windu, Ki-Adi-Mundi, and Yoda met with the Chancellor to discuss an upcoming vote in the Senate that would plunge the Republic into war with the Separatists.

"You must realize there are not enough Jedi to defend the Republic," Mace cautioned Palpatine. "We are keepers of the peace, not soldiers."

Senator Amidala entered the Chancellor's chamber. She suspected

Count Dooku, the mysterious leader of the Separatists, was behind the attack on her life, but the Jedi Council wasn't so sure.

Regardless, Chancellor Palpatine was concerned for Padmé's safety.

"Master Jedi, may I suggest the senator be placed under your protection?"

Padmé protested, but the Jedi agreed with the Chancellor.

Obi-Wan Kenobi and his Padawan, Anakin Skywalker, arrived to help protect the senator. The young Jedi was eager to determine who was threatening Padmé's life.

Obi-Wan reminded Anakin, "We're here to protect her, not start an investigation."

But Anakin was too excited to see Padmé again to listen. It had been ten years since they had last seen each other.

"Ani?" Padmé asked.

She barely recognized the young boy she had met on Tatooine all those years before.

Obi-Wan and Anakin's fears about Padmé's safety were confirmed that very evening. An assassin sent a robotic attack droid, armed with deadly insects, into her room to poison her!

Fortunately, the Jedi sensed the evil mission in time to interfere. Obi-Wan grabbed on to the floating droid as it fled the scene and was soon hanging on for dear life as it flew over the streets of Coruscant.

Anakin jumped into a speeder to rescue Obi-Wan and follow the droid.

They needed to find out who had set up the deadly scheme.

From their speeder, Obi-Wan and Anakin spotted Zam, a bounty hunter assassin. Was she behind the attack?

Anakin navigated the heavy traffic of Coruscant, but Zam managed to slip away.

Obi-Wan was frustrated with Anakin as they floated high above the city.

"Well, you've lost her."

Or so he thought! Anakin was waiting for Zam to come out of a tunnel. When she did, Anakin prepared to jump out of the speeder.

"Excuse me for a moment."

Obi-Wan watched in horror as Anakin dropped straight toward the street! Using his Jedi skills, Anakin landed on Zam's speeder, causing the vehicle to wobble and crash.

Obi-Wan met his apprentice on the ground, and the Jedi tried to get answers from the shape-shifting assassin, but she was hit by another bounty hunter's poisonous dart before she could tell them anything.

Ambushed!

Obi-Wan and Anakin told the Jedi Council what had happened.

"Track down this bounty hunter, you must, Obi-Wan," urged Yoda.

But Obi-Wan was concerned about Padmé's safety; who would protect her if he was looking for the bounty hunter?

"Handle that, your Padawan will," replied Yoda.

"Anakin, escort the senator back to her home planet of Naboo," Mace Windu instructed.

It was clear Padmé was no longer safe on Coruscant.

Anakin was delighted by his new assignment.

He had missed spending time with his friend Padmé.

As the two departed on their journey with their faithful droid, R2-D2, Padmé turned to Anakin.

"Suddenly, I'm afraid."

"I am, too," Anakin confessed. But he was determined to lift her spirits. "Don't worry, we've got Artoo with us."

Anakin and Padmé were destined to grow closer as their adventure continued.

THE SECRET ARMY

Jedi Master Obi-Wan Kenobi had a problem. Someone was trying to hurt Senator Amidala. But the Jedi Council couldn't figure out who it was. The only clue they had was a poisonous dart the enemy had used—a very strange-looking dart.

Obi-Wan decided to ask his friend Dexter Jettster for help. He might know where the dart had come from. After all, Dex had a way of knowing about things that were . . . out of the ordinary.

"What you got here is a Kamino saberdart," Dex told Obi-Wan.

"Kamino?" asked Obi-Wan.

Dex nodded. "It's a planet beyond the Outer Rim. The folks there keep to themselves. They're cloners."

Obi-Wan had never heard of Kamino. So he went to research it in the Jedi Archives.

But to his surprise, the planet didn't show up in the map charts.

"Are you sure you have the right coordinates?" the archive keeper asked him.

"Yes," said Obi-Wan. "It should appear right here, just south of the Rishi Maze."

The keeper shook her head. "I hate to say it, but if an item does not appear in our records, it does not exist."

The mystery was becoming stranger and stranger. Obi-Wan had to get to the bottom of it.

And that meant asking the wisest Jedi he knew for help: Master Yoda.

Obi-Wan found the old master training a class of young Padawans.

"Hmmmm. Lost a planet, Master Obi-Wan has," Yoda said to his students. "How embarrassing."

The children giggled.

Yoda pulled up a 3D map of the galaxy. Obi-Wan pointed to where the planet should have been. "Gravity is pulling all the stars in the area to this spot," he said. "But the planet isn't there."

"Master?" A very small boy raised his hand. "Perhaps someone erased it from the archive memory?"

Yoda nodded proudly. "Truly wonderful the mind of a child is. The Padawan is right. Go to the center of gravity's pull, and find your planet, you will."

Obi-Wan was growing worried. Only a Jedi could have erased those files from the archives. But who? And why?

Quickly, he flew to the coordinates Dex had given him. Sure enough, there was the planet Kamino!

Obi-Wan landed his starship on the platform of a large spaceport. To his surprise, a tall alien named Taun We came out to greet him.

"Master Jedi," she said, "the prime minister is expecting you."

"I'm expected?" Obi-Wan raised his eyebrows.

"Of course," Taun We said. "He is anxious to meet you. After all these years, we were beginning to think you weren't coming."

Taun We took Obi-Wan to meet the Kamino prime minister, Lama Su.

"You will be delighted to hear we are on schedule," Lama Su told Obi-Wan. "Two hundred thousand units are ready, with a million more on the way. Please tell your master, Sifo-Dyas, that his order will be met on time."

Obi-Wan was extremely confused. "Master Sifo-Dyas was killed almost ten years ago."

Lama Su was surprised. "I'm so sorry to hear that. But I'm sure he would have been proud of the clone army we've built for him."

Obi-Wan had no idea what Lama Su was talking about. But he decided to play along. "Tell me, when my Master first contacted you, did he say who the army was for?"

"The Jedi Council requested this army for the Republic," Lama Su replied.

Taun We and Lama Su took Obi-Wan to see the clone army. Obi-Wan couldn't believe his eyes. There were thousands and thousands of clone soldiers in the spaceport—eating, exercising, training. And they all looked exactly the same.

"They are totally obedient," Lama Su explained proudly, "taking any order without question. We modified their genetic structure to make them less independent than the original host."

"And who is the original host?" Obi-Wan asked.

"A bounty hunter called Jango Fett," said Lama Su.

A bounty hunter! thought Obi-Wan. *That could be the culprit behind the attacks on Senator Amidala.* He asked to meet Jango Fett.

"This is Jedi Master Obi-Wan Kenobi," Taun We said, introducing Obi-Wan to Jango Fett and his clone son, Boba.

"Tell me, have you ever been to Coruscant?" Obi-Wan asked Jango.

"Once or twice," Jango replied warily.

Obi-Wan got a very bad feeling about Jango. He was certain he'd found the mysterious attacker they were looking for.

Obi-Wan needed to tell Yoda and Mace Windu what he had discovered. He hurried back to his ship and sent them a message.

"The Kaminos are using a bounty hunter named Jango Fett to create a clone army," Obi-Wan said. "I have a strong feeling that this bounty hunter is the assassin we're looking for."

"An army?" Master Yoda asked.

"Yes," said Obi-Wan. "The Kamino prime minister said that the Jedi Council placed an order for a clone army almost ten years ago. Is that true?"

"No," said Mace Windu.

"Bring the bounty hunter here," said Yoda. "Question him, we will."

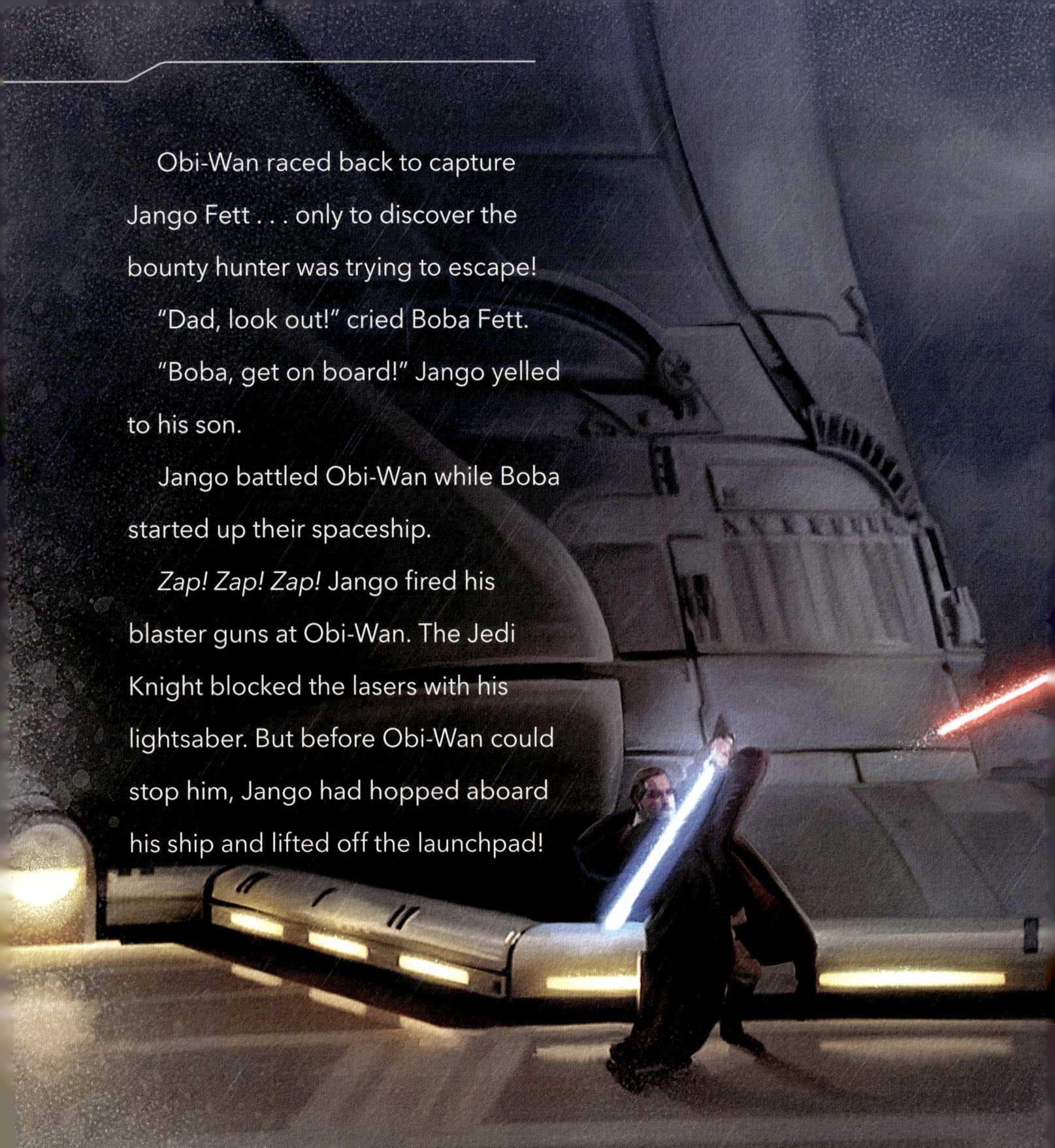

Obi-Wan raced back to capture Jango Fett . . . only to discover the bounty hunter was trying to escape!

"Dad, look out!" cried Boba Fett.

"Boba, get on board!" Jango yelled to his son.

Jango battled Obi-Wan while Boba started up their spaceship.

Zap! Zap! Zap! Jango fired his blaster guns at Obi-Wan. The Jedi Knight blocked the lasers with his lightsaber. But before Obi-Wan could stop him, Jango had hopped aboard his ship and lifted off the launchpad!

Thinking fast, Obi-Wan threw a tracking device at Jango's ship.

SNAP! It attached to the hull just in time. The ship took off and blasted into space!

Phew, Obi-Wan thought. *At least now I can track him.*

No matter where the bounty hunter went, Obi-Wan would follow him and get to the bottom of the mystery once and for all!

ANAKIN'S VOW

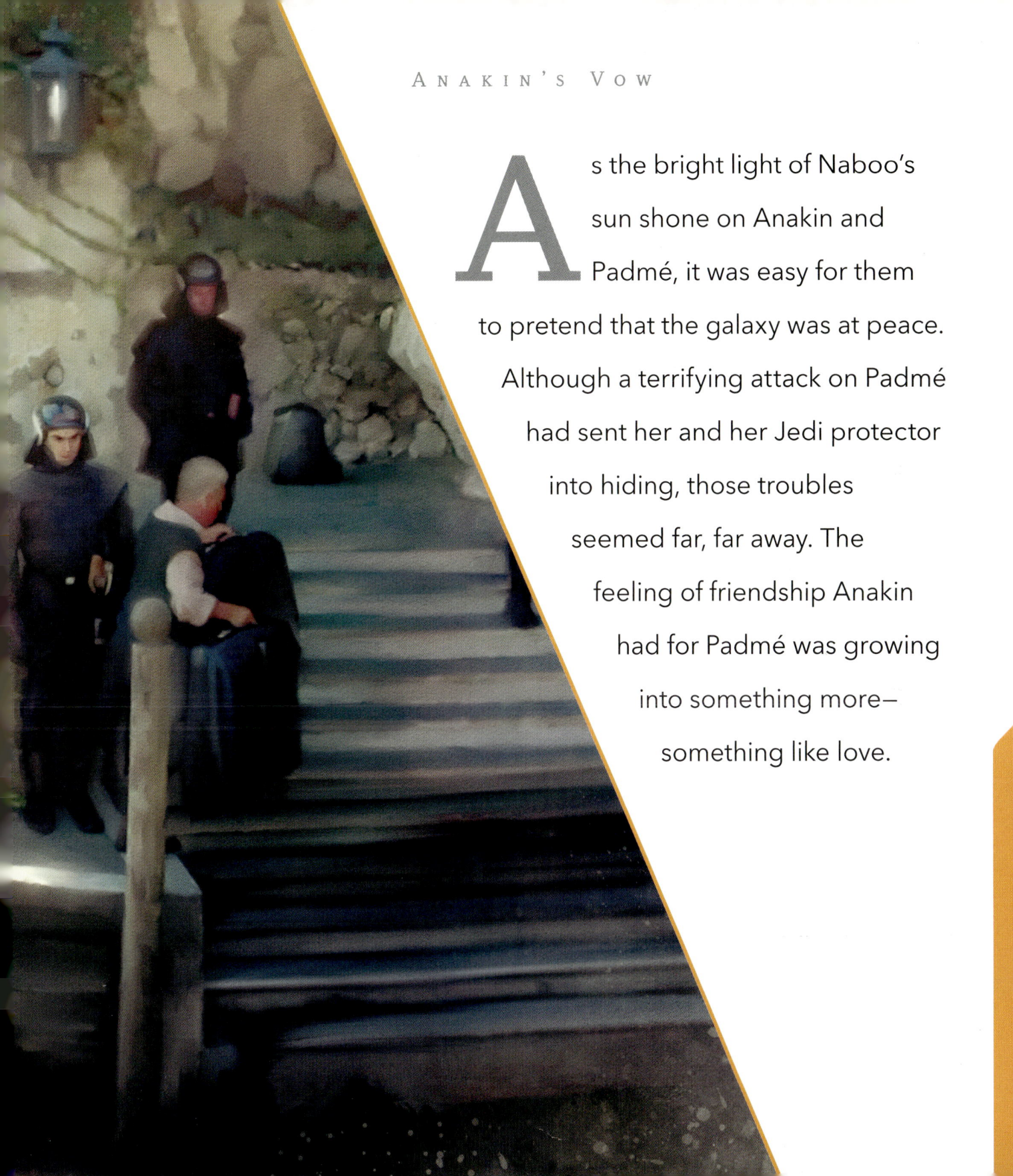

ANAKIN'S VOW

As the bright light of Naboo's sun shone on Anakin and Padmé, it was easy for them to pretend that the galaxy was at peace. Although a terrifying attack on Padmé had sent her and her Jedi protector into hiding, those troubles seemed far, far away. The feeling of friendship Anakin had for Padmé was growing into something more—something like love.

Anakin and Padmé spent their days exploring the beautiful waterfalls and valleys of the countryside. But even though everything around Anakin was peaceful, something felt wrong. Every night he had the same nightmare. He tossed and turned as visions of his mother, Shmi, haunted his dreams. Somehow he knew she was in trouble.

Finally, Anakin couldn't ignore the dreams any longer. "I have to go. I have to help her," Anakin told Padmé.

"I'll go with you," she promised.

So together, the senator and the Jedi traveled to Tatooine in search of Anakin's mother. Anakin had not been back to his home planet since he was a little boy. He was so different. He wondered if his planet had changed, too.

STAR WARS STORYBOOK COLLECTION

The two began their quest by finding someone Anakin knew well . . . unfortunately. Watto, the junk dealer, had never been kind to Anakin as a child, but he was their best chance of finding Anakin's mother.

Watto greeted Anakin with disbelief. "Little Ani? You sure sprouted, huh. A Jedi! Whaddya know?"

Watto explained that Shmi had moved away and married a farmer named Cliegg Lars.

It didn't take long for Anakin and Padmé to track down Cliegg on his moisture farm in the desert. They even found the droid Anakin had built as a child—C-3PO!

"I knew you would return. I knew it!" the droid gushed.

But Cliegg had terrible news for Anakin. Shmi had been captured by Tusken Raiders over a month before. There was little hope that she was still alive.

Anakin refused to give up on his mother. He grabbed a speeder and raced through the desert, far into the Tusken Raiders' territory. Even though he knew a Jedi should be calm and patient, fear had pushed every other thought out of Anakin's mind. He had to find his mother before it was too late.

Soon Anakin discovered the Tusken Raiders' camp. He snuck silently from tent to tent until he found the one that held his mother. She had been tied up and left alone with no one to help her. Shmi was badly hurt. Anakin knew she would never make it back home with him.

Anakin held his mother in his arms one last time.

"I'm so proud of you, Ani," Shmi said.

Her message delivered, Anakin's mother let go of her pain and became one with the Force.

But even though Shmi was at peace, Anakin was not. A burning rage filled him as he thought of the Tusken Raiders who had hurt his mother. Anakin drew his lightsaber and gave in to his anger. He stormed through the camp, destroying everything in his way.

Later, back at Cliegg's home, Anakin told Padmé about what had happened. Hurting the Tusken Raiders hadn't made Anakin feel any better. Anakin never wanted to feel so sad and angry again. He made a promise to himself and to Padmé.

"Someday I will be the most powerful Jedi ever," he said. "I will even learn to stop people from dying."

STAR WARS STORYBOOK COLLECTION

Anakin, Padmé, Cliegg, and his family gathered outside to pay their last respects to Shmi. Anakin felt the rage returning again, but this time he channeled the anger toward his new goal. He would never again let anything bad happen to someone he loved.

Anakin's fear and anger were leading him down a dark path, but the young Jedi had vowed to follow that path—no matter where it led.

A DEADLY PLOT

A Deadly Plot

Two ships whizzed through an asteroid field. They were piloted by Obi-Wan Kenobi and Jango Fett!

Obi-Wan was chasing Jango and his clone son, Boba, to take them back to the Jedi Council for questioning. But the dangerous bounty hunter wasn't going down without a fight.

Jango Fett launched a torpedo at Obi-Wan's ship.

KA-BOOM! There was a giant explosion.

"Well, we won't be seeing him again." Jango laughed.

But Obi-Wan had released a canister of spare parts for the torpedo to hit. Obi-Wan piloted his ship behind an asteroid and hid there while Jango's ship passed. Then he stealthily flew after him.

Jango landed on a nearby planet called Geonosis. He and Boba climbed down from the ship and headed into a massive hall built right into the rock of the planet.

Obi-Wan carefully followed the bounty hunter's trail.

As he went, Obi-Wan could scarcely believe his eyes. Hundreds of Trade Federation ships were docked on the planet, with even more in the sky. And the towers engineered into the planet's surface looked like work factories.

Something bad was happening there—something very bad.

Inside the factory, Obi-Wan's worst fears were confirmed.

Geonosian workers were building thousands and thousands of battle droids.

The Trade Federation was creating an army to destroy the Jedi . . . and the entire Republic!

Suddenly, Obi-Wan heard voices.

From his hiding spot, Obi-Wan watched as a group of Separatist leaders gathered. An older man with a crooked nose addressed them all.

Obi-Wan knew the man. He was a powerful former Jedi.

Count Dooku.

"With the battle droids we have built, we shall have an army greater than anything in the galaxy," Count Dooku said.

A Deadly Plot

Obi-Wan needed to warn the Jedi Council!

"I have tracked Jango Fett to Geonosis," Obi-Wan recorded. "Viceroy Gunray is behind the assassination attempts on Senator Amidala. The Separatists have pledged their droid armies to Count Dooku and are forming a—"

Suddenly, a battle droid attacked the Jedi and knocked him unconscious! Obi-Wan's droid, R4, sent the partial message to the Council just in time.

When Obi-Wan awoke, he was trapped in a stasis field. Count Dooku was circling him.

"Traitor," Obi-Wan said.

"Oh, no, my friend," insisted Count Dooku. "I am not the enemy. What if I told you that the Republic is under the influence of a Sith Lord called Darth Sidious? That is the villain we Separatists are trying to stop! You must join me, Obi-Wan, and together we will destroy the Sith."

But Obi-Wan didn't believe Dooku. "I will never join you."

Back on Coruscant, the Jedi Council reviewed Obi-Wan's partial message.

"More happening on Geonosis, I feel, than has been revealed," said Yoda.

They needed to rescue Obi-Wan.

"Now we need that clone army, to defend the Republic against the

A Deadly Plot

droids," another Jedi said. "But the Senate will never approve it."

"The Senate must vote to give Chancellor Palpatine emergency powers!" exclaimed another. "He could approve the use of the clones."

"But what senator would have the courage to propose such a radical amendment?" asked Chancellor Palpatine.

In the corner of the room, Jar Jar Binks took a deep breath. Senator Amidala had left him in charge as her representative. He knew what he had to do.

The next day, Jar Jar Binks addressed the Senate. "In response to the direct threat to the Republic, mesa propose that the Senate give immediately emergency powers to the Supreme Chancellor!"

Thunderous cheers echoed throughout the hall. All the senators agreed. This was an emergency.

Chancellor Palpatine stood. "The power you give me I will lay down when this crisis has ended, I promise you. As my first act with this new authority, I will create a grand army of the Republic to counter the increasing threats of the Separatists."

The entire Senate chamber burst into thunderous applause.

High above on a balcony, Jedi Masters Yoda and Mace Windu watched.

"It is done, then," said Mace Windu.

Though the Jedi had never intended to create a clone army, the Republic would use it to battle the Separatists and their droid soldiers.

Yoda and Mace Windu just hoped they wouldn't come to regret that decision.

INTO THE ARENA

INTO THE ARENA

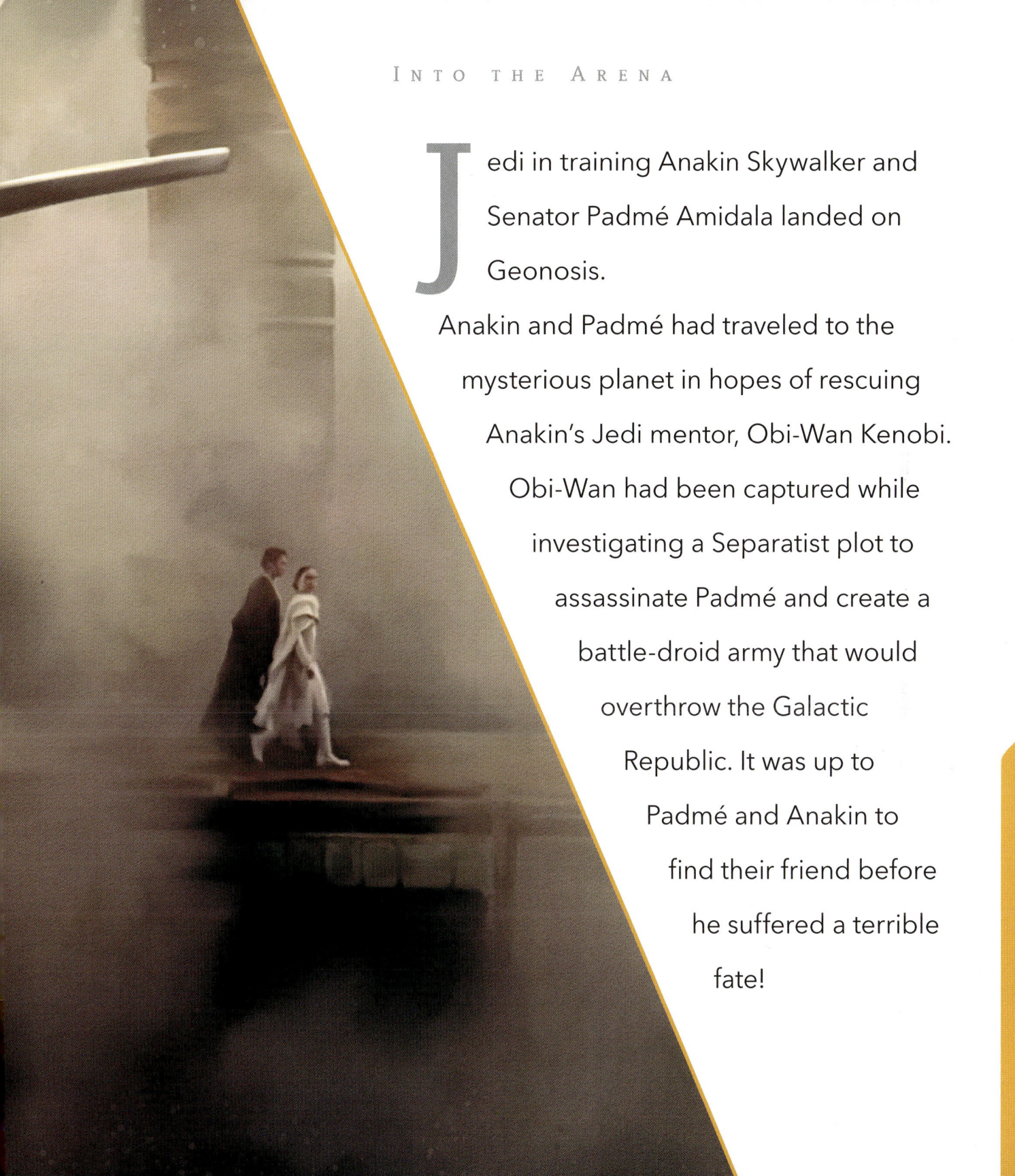

Jedi in training Anakin Skywalker and Senator Padmé Amidala landed on Geonosis. Anakin and Padmé had traveled to the mysterious planet in hopes of rescuing Anakin's Jedi mentor, Obi-Wan Kenobi. Obi-Wan had been captured while investigating a Separatist plot to assassinate Padmé and create a battle-droid army that would overthrow the Galactic Republic. It was up to Padmé and Anakin to find their friend before he suffered a terrible fate!

As Anakin and Padmé headed down a long pathway, winged creatures suddenly began to attack them! Lightsaber blazing, Anakin cut down the creatures as he and Padmé headed for safety. However, they soon found themselves on a short walkway extending over a maze of machinery.

Suddenly, the door behind them closed and the walkway started to retract. Padmé had no choice but to jump down onto one of the many conveyor belts that filled the droid factory and duck and dodge the dangerous machinery.

"Padmé!" the young Jedi shouted as he leapt down after her, using his lightsaber to disable the mechanical arms that grabbed for him.

Despite their heroic efforts, the pair were finally captured—Padmé by the winged creatures and Anakin by a group of destroyer droids.

Suddenly, an armored figure dropped from above, blaster in hand.

"Don't move!" he shouted. It was Jango Fett, the armored bounty hunter working for the Separatists!

STAR WARS STORYBOOK COLLECTION

As Anakin and Padmé awaited their fate, Anakin worried that Padmé was afraid.

"I'm not afraid to die," she said. "I've been dying a little bit each day since you came back into my life. . . . I love you."

"You love me?" Anakin was shocked, as Padmé had always said they could never be together.

"I truly, deeply love you," she replied.

The young couple strained against their bonds to share a kiss, just before they were carried out into a vast arena.

The crowd cheered as Anakin and Padmé were taken to the center of the arena and chained to posts alongside Obi-Wan Kenobi.

High above, Count Dooku and Jango Fett looked on as a thunderous announcement rang out across the arena: "Let the executions begin!"

Three large gates opened, and monstrous creatures—a giant bull of a reek, a catlike nexu, and a clawed beast called an acklay—were herded into the arena by spear-carrying guards. The trio of beasts began charging toward the prisoners, each choosing a specific target!

"I've got a bad feeling about this," said Anakin.

Obi-Wan urged calm to his Jedi apprentice, but Anakin was worried about Padmé—who had been targeted by the nexu—at least until he saw that she had already freed one of her hands, using a bit of wire she had hidden before their capture. Still trapped by a length of chain attached to one wrist, she had climbed to the top of her post, playing a game of cat and mouse as she landed swift blows on the nexu with her restraints.

As for Anakin, he used his Jedi training to evade the reek long enough to turn his chain into reins that could steer the giant beast.

Meanwhile, Obi-Wan used the acklay's charging attack to his advantage, freeing himself just before the beast knocked down his post! Quickly grabbing one of the guards' herding spears, he faced off against the monster!

Padmé, having managed to pull free from her chain, climbed on top of the reek with Anakin. Obi-Wan joined them once he had managed to disable the acklay.

But Count Dooku wouldn't let the three friends go so easily. He sent destroyer droids to surround Padmé and the Jedi.

Unnoticed during all the uproar, Jedi Master Mace Windu had arrived on Geonosis. He confronted Count Dooku and Jango Fett.

"This party's over," said Mace as one hundred Jedi Knights—who had taken strategic positions throughout the arena—revealed themselves by igniting their lightsabers.

Count Dooku sneered at the Jedi.

"Brave but foolish, my old friend," he said. "You're impossibly outnumbered."

In an instant, thousands of droids began to pour into the arena!

Frightened by the droids' sudden appearance, the remaining creatures began stampeding around the arena, trampling anyone in their path. Anakin, Padmé, Obi-Wan, and Mace Windu joined the fight between the Jedi and the droids, and the chaos quickly grew.

Back to back, with their lightsabers ablaze, Mace and Obi-Wan bravely defeated dozens and dozens of droids, but for every droid soldier they cut down, two others seemed to appear.

It began to look as though even the Force would not be enough to save them this time.

THE BRINK OF WAR

THE BRINK OF WAR

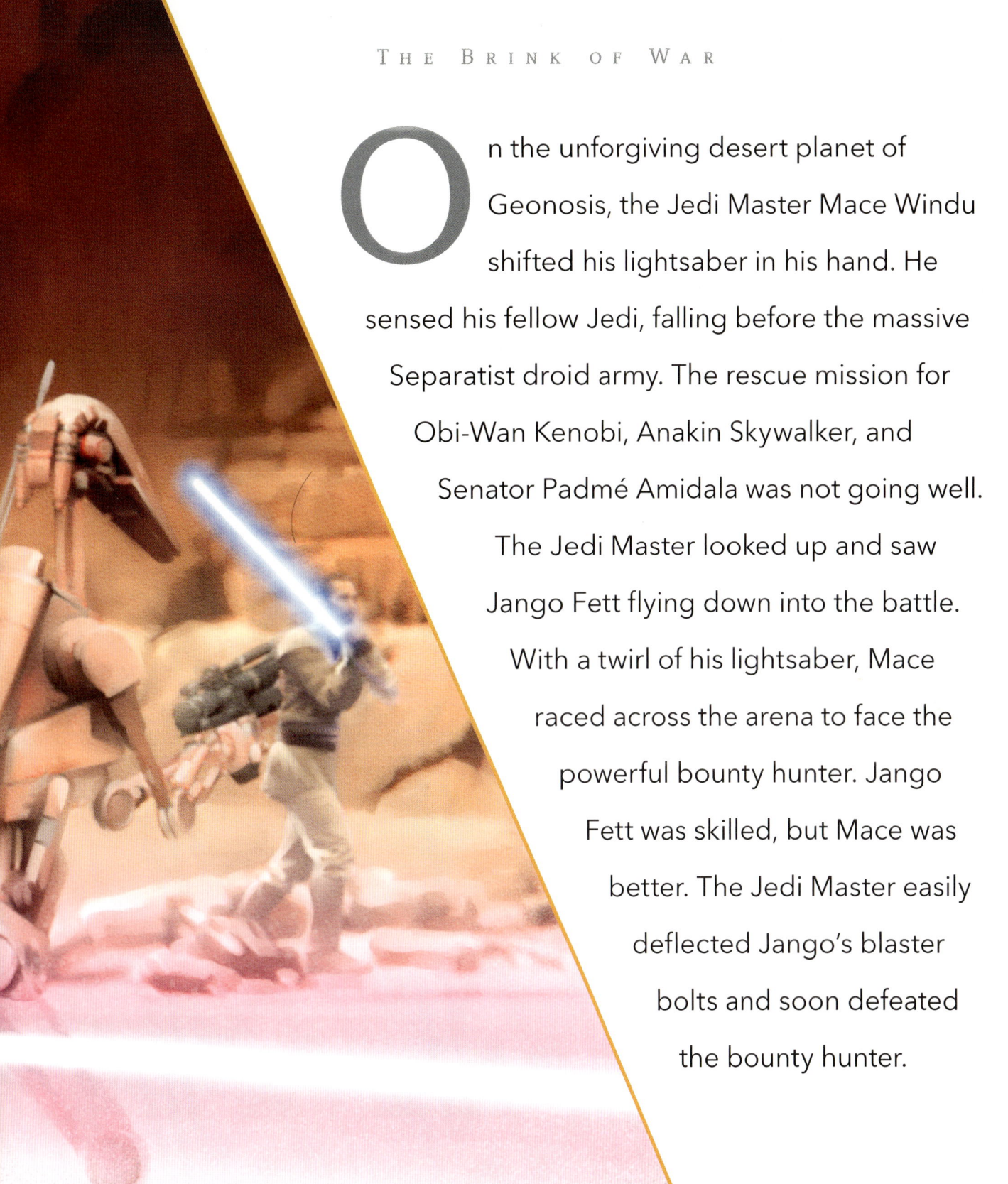

On the unforgiving desert planet of Geonosis, the Jedi Master Mace Windu shifted his lightsaber in his hand. He sensed his fellow Jedi, falling before the massive Separatist droid army. The rescue mission for Obi-Wan Kenobi, Anakin Skywalker, and Senator Padmé Amidala was not going well. The Jedi Master looked up and saw Jango Fett flying down into the battle. With a twirl of his lightsaber, Mace raced across the arena to face the powerful bounty hunter. Jango Fett was skilled, but Mace was better. The Jedi Master easily deflected Jango's blaster bolts and soon defeated the bounty hunter.

But Mace's victory came too late. He fell back to join the small circle of remaining Jedi. There were so few, and the Separatist droid army just kept coming. The Separatist leader, Count Dooku, spoke from a high balcony.

"Mace Windu! You have fought gallantly, worthy of recognition in the archives of the Jedi Order. Now it is finished. Surrender, and your lives will be spared."

But Master Windu refused. He would not allow his fellow Jedi to become hostages for the Separatists to use against the Republic. The battle would end there.

"Look!" Padmé yelled, breaking the standoff. Everyone looked up to see a new player ready to join the fight. It was the clone army—a force that Obi-Wan had only recently discovered and that had been secretly created for the Republic's use. At its head was Master Yoda!

"Around the survivors a perimeter create," the Jedi Master commanded his generals from a ship high above the fray.

STAR WARS STORYBOOK COLLECTION

Mace Windu ordered the Jedi to jump onto the ships as the clone army began its attack on the Separatists. The ships flew away from the arena and over Geonosis. Huge battle droids were clashing with the clone army war machines. Blaster fire rained down as massive ships fought for control of the desert planet. Mace realized that the battle was close to becoming a war.

THE BRINK OF WAR

Master Yoda looked over at Mace. "If Dooku escapes, rally more systems to his cause he will."

Mace nodded. They had to find the Separatist leader. It was their only chance of ending the war before it began.

Count Dooku, however, was far out of reach of Mace Windu. But like his Jedi enemy, the Count was thinking about the future.

"The Jedi must not find our ultimate weapon," a Geonosian leader urged. "If they find out what we are planning to build we're doomed."

"I will take the designs with me to Coruscant," Count Dooku said. "They will be much safer there with my master." He pocketed the plans, knowing victory would be ensured if he could get off the planet.

THE BRINK OF WAR

But Obi-Wan Kenobi and Anakin Skywalker were determined to stop the Count in his tracks.

"You're going to pay for all the Jedi that you killed today, Dooku," said Anakin as he raced toward the Count with his lightsaber raised.

"Brave of you, boy," Count Dooku said.

The foes flew across the room, battling it out. But Anakin still had much to learn, and not even the seasoned Jedi Master Obi-Wan Kenobi could defeat Count Dooku.

But there was another Jedi waiting in the wings.

It was Master Yoda.

"You have interfered with our affairs for the last time," Dooku said, sending rocks, heavy metal towers, and even Force lightning at the old Jedi.

"Much to learn you still have," Yoda told Dooku as he swatted aside each projectile.

"It is obvious that this contest cannot be decided by our knowledge of the Force, but by our skills with a lightsaber," Dooku replied.

The Separatist leader leapt across the room toward the Jedi Master. Yoda's blade clashed again the Count's. Wherever Dooku's blade was, so was Yoda's. It was impossible for Dooku to create an opening.

"Fought well, you have, my old Padawan," Yoda said.

"This is just the beginning," Count Dooku told his old master. He broke away from the battle and reached his hand toward a large tower. It began to fall down, right on Obi-Wan and Anakin!

Yoda had no choice but to save his fellow Jedi. He sensed Dooku escaping as he used the Force to move the giant tower safely away from Obi-Wan and Anakin. War with the Separatists was inevitable.

Count Dooku flew away from Geonosis and safely back to his master.

"The Force is with us, Master Sidious," he told the powerful Sith.

Count Dooku handed Darth Sidious the plans for the ultimate weapon. Once it was built, there would be little hope for the Republic.

STAR WARS STORYBOOK COLLECTION

With Geonosis won, what was left of the Jedi forces regrouped on Coruscant.

"I have to admit," Obi-Wan told Mace Windu and Master Yoda, "that without the clones, it would not have been a victory."

THE BRINK OF WAR

"Victory?" Yoda said. "Victory, you say? Master Obi-Wan, not victory. The shroud of the dark side has fallen. Begun, the Clone War has."

Master Yoda was right to worry. Count Dooku was missing, and the Jedi forces were weakened from the battle at Geonosis. Instead of leading missions of peace, the Jedi would be responsible for leading troops of warriors.

As the leader of the Senate, Chancellor Palpatine was now the head of a vast and powerful army. Yoda hoped he would use his power well and that peace would once again return to the galaxy.

STAR WARS STORYBOOK COLLECTION

And for one brief moment it did. In a secret ceremony, far away from any army—clone or droid—Anakin and Padmé were married. Now more than ever, the future was uncertain. But both the Jedi and the senator knew that together they were stronger. Together, they could face anything.

The Duel with Dooku

The Galactic Republic was crumbling under attacks from the ruthless Sith Lord Count Dooku. In a stunning move, Dooku and the fiendish cyborg leader General Grievous had kidnapped Chancellor Palpatine, leader of the Galactic Senate. But while the Separatist droid army attempted to flee with its valuable hostage, Jedi Knights Obi-Wan Kenobi and Anakin Skywalker undertook a risky mission to rescue the Chancellor. In their ships, Obi-Wan and Anakin battled through a swarm of deadly droid fighters until Anakin's incredible skill as a pilot enabled them to successfully reach Count Dooku's command vessel, a Trade Federation cruiser.

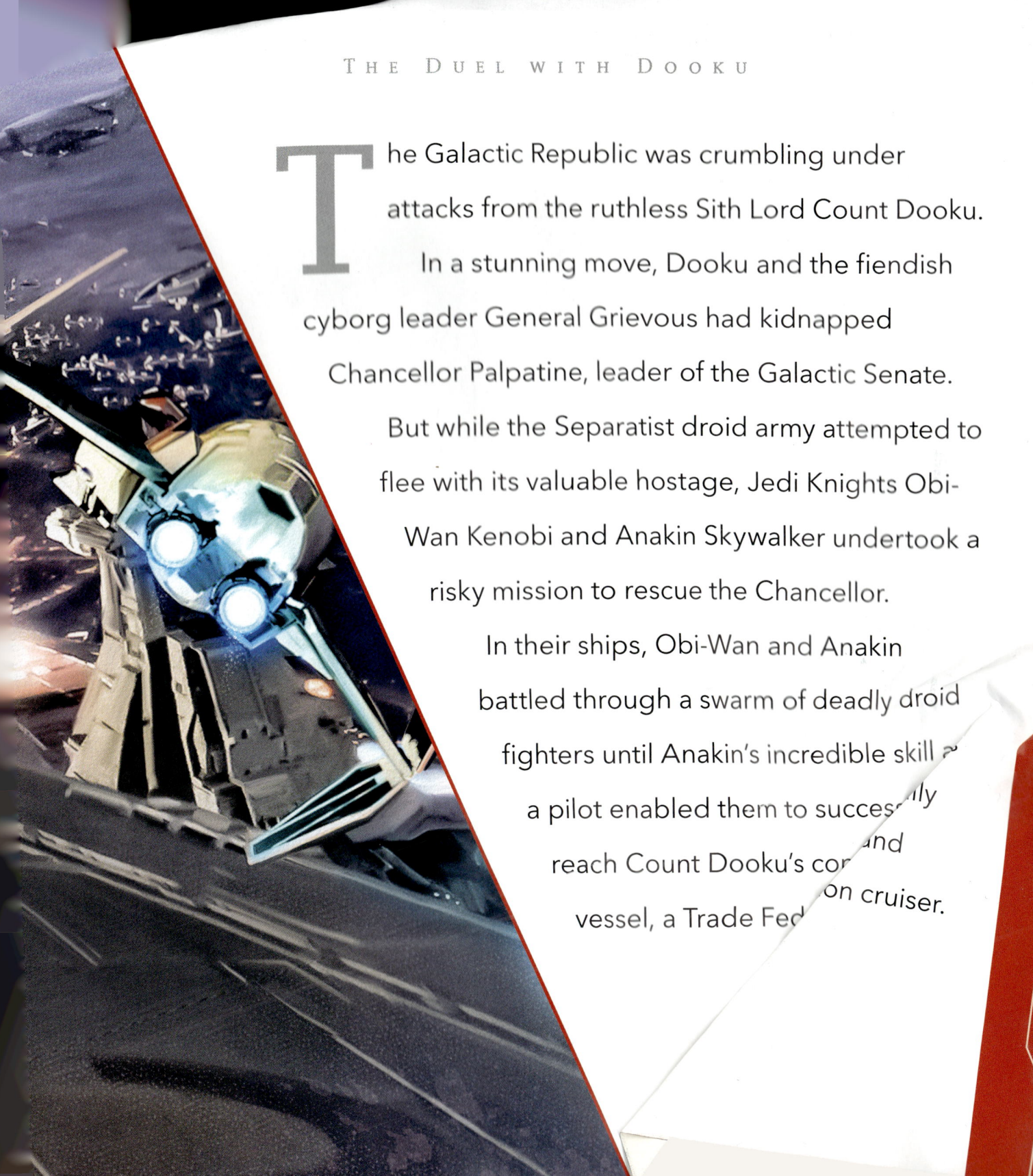

Suddenly, Anakin and Obi-Wan were attacked by battle droids coming at them from all directions! Lightsabers flashing, the Jedi defeated them swiftly.

R2-D2 accessed the cruiser's computers and discovered that Chancellor Palpatine was being held prisoner on an observation platform many levels away.

Leaving R2 to guard Anakin's ship, the Jedi Knights made their way to the Chancellor's location.

"I see Count Dooku," said Anakin.

"I sense a trap," replied Obi-Wan, and he was right. General Grievous was tracking their every move!

With a little help from R2-D2, the Jedi soon found themselves face to face with Chancellor Palpatine. However, they were also in the presence of Count Dooku!

"You're no match for him," said the Chancellor, urging the Jedi to call for help. "He's a Sith Lord."

Smiling, Obi-Wan replied, "Chancellor Palpatine, Sith Lords are our specialty."

The Jedi Knights ignited their lightsabers, but Dooku parried their every attack.

"I've been looking forward to this," gloated Dooku.

"My powers have doubled since the last time we met," Anakin replied.

Using the Force, Dooku sent Obi-Wan flying. The Jedi Knight was knocked unconscious. It would be up to Anakin to defeat Dooku alone, but the Sith Lord was confident *he* would be the victor.

"I sense great fear in you," said the Sith Lord to his opponent. "You have hate, you have anger, but you don't use them."

Anakin attacked the Count with even greater ferocity. He was stronger than Dooku, and soon the Count was on his knees, begging for mercy.

Chancellor Palpatine encouraged Anakin to end the battle and kill the Separatist leader.

Killing an unarmed prisoner was not the Jedi way, and the young Skywalker was uncertain what to do. "I shouldn't . . ." he said, hesitating, but Palpatine urged him on.

Anakin yielded to Palpatine's request, and defeated Dooku.

"It's only natural," Palpatine reassured the Jedi. "You wanted revenge. . . . Now we must leave before more security droids arrive."

But Anakin wouldn't leave without Obi-Wan.

"Leave him, or we'll never make it," urged Palpatine.

"His fate will be the same as ours," replied a defiant Anakin, lifting the unconscious Obi-Wan over his shoulder.

Damaged by the clone army's assault, the cruiser was beginning to drift in space.

Obi-Wan stirred as the group neared the hangar, but soon the group was boxed in by ray shields, unable to move.

"How did this happen?" Obi-Wan asked, disappointed in Anakin's rescue attempt.

Anakin tried to reassure his mentor. "Artoo will be along in a few moments. He'll release the ray shields."

R2-D2 did arrive shortly, but he was followed by dozens of enemy droids, who took the rescue party and Palpatine to the evil General Grievous.

"Do you have a plan B?" asked Obi-Wan.

Grievous, holding both Jedi's lightsabers, taunted his prisoners: "That wasn't much of a rescue."

Obi-Wan ignored the insult.

"We have a job to do," the Jedi Master explained as he used the Force to summon his lightsaber from Grievous's hand, and then he swiftly freed himself and Anakin from their restraints.

They quickly defeated the battle droids, but Grievous managed to slip away and flee the damaged cruiser in an escape pod!

As the ship's alarms began to ring, the Jedi Knights realized that there was no way to get back to their ship. And what was worse, General Grievous had launched all the cruiser's escape pods, meaning they had only one slim chance of survival.

"Can you fly a cruiser like this?" Obi-Wan asked Anakin.

"You mean do I know how to land what's left of it?" the young Jedi countered. "Strap yourselves in."

Anakin took the pilot's chair as the ship plummeted toward Coruscant!

STAR WARS STORYBOOK COLLECTION

With pieces flying off the burning ship as it entered Coruscant's atmosphere, Anakin steered his way toward an industrial landing strip. In a cloud of fire and smoke, the wrecked vehicle touched down roughly, leaving the Jedi Knights and the Chancellor safe at last!

"Another happy landing," Obi-Wan said with a sigh.

THE CYBORG AND THE JEDI

THE CYBORG AND THE JEDI

At the edge of the galaxy, the fearsome cyborg General Grievous was on the run from the Jedi and their clone army.

After his attempt to kidnap the leader of the Senate had failed, General Grievous and his droid army had retreated to Utapau. The remote planet was the perfect place to hide while he waited for instructions from his master, Darth Sidious.

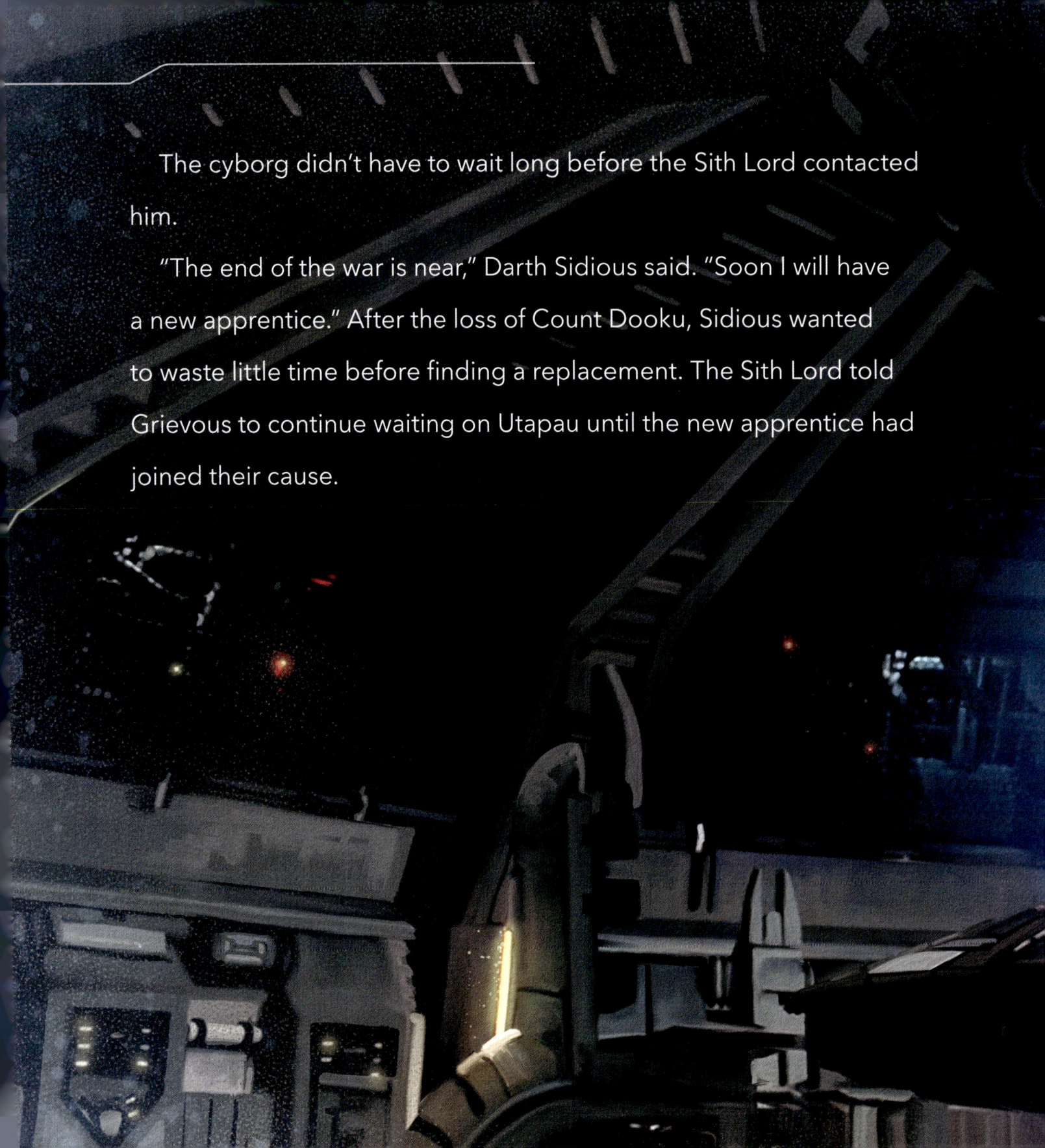

The cyborg didn't have to wait long before the Sith Lord contacted him.

"The end of the war is near," Darth Sidious said. "Soon I will have a new apprentice." After the loss of Count Dooku, Sidious wanted to waste little time before finding a replacement. The Sith Lord told Grievous to continue waiting on Utapau until the new apprentice had joined their cause.

But the Jedi Council had discovered that Grievous and his droid army were on Utapau. Like Sidious, the Jedi believed the war would end soon—if only they could capture General Grievous. So the Jedi sent Obi-Wan and a platoon of clone troopers to drive out Grievous and destroy his army once and for all.

Obi-Wan met with his men before the battle and gave them their orders. Obi-Wan would fly ahead and keep Grievous from escaping. Then the clone troopers would land and take care of Grievous's army.

When Obi-Wan landed on Utapau, he didn't have to look far to find Grievous. A Pau'an leader met Obi-Wan at his ship and leaned in close.

"He is here! They are watching us," the man whispered. "The tenth level . . . thousands of battle droids . . ."

Obi-Wan instructed the Pau'an to tell his people to take shelter.

Obi-Wan mounted a feathery varactyl and set off to confront Grievous. Just as the Pau'an had said, the tenth level was swarming with droids—and their evil leader was at the center of it all. The Jedi and the cyborg had fought each other once before, but Obi-Wan wasn't going to let Grievous escape this time. Obi-Wan took off his bulky robe and leapt out of the shadows.

"Hello, there," Obi-Wan said with a tight smile.

"General Kenobi." Grievous laughed. "You are a bold one."

Obi-Wan quickly drew his lightsaber and cut down Grievous's guard droids.

"You fool. I have been trained in your Jedi arts," Grievous said. The cyborg extended his four arms, revealing that each one held a lightsaber. Obi-Wan heard the snap-hiss of the blades igniting as Grievous stomped forward, spinning two of the blades above his head. He dragged the other two along the ground, sending sparks hurtling toward Obi-Wan.

The Jedi waited for the perfect moment, then stabbed his lightsaber between Grievous's flashing blades.

Obi-Wan cut through two of Grievous's lightsabers, disarming half of the cyborg's deadly weapons. Obi-Wan pressed his advantage, driving Grievous back farther and farther.

The droids watched as their leader lost more and more ground. But before they could help Grievous fight back, a hail of blaster bolts filled the air. The clone troopers had arrived!

"Army or not, you must realize you're doomed," Grievous said.

"Oh, I don't think so," Obi-Wan replied. He used the Force to push Grievous up against a wall, causing the cyborg to drop his remaining two lightsabers.

Grievous tried to run away by jumping on board a wheel bike. But Obi-Wan's varactyl friend was still nearby. Obi-Wan leapt onto the speedy beast and raced after Grievous.

The Jedi urged his varactyl as close as he could to Grievous's speeding bike and jumped on board. Grievous attempted to defend himself with an electrostaff and a blaster, but Obi-Wan tipped the bike over, spilling Obi-Wan, Grievous, and his weapons onto a small landing pad.

Grievous grabbed the electrostaff and forced Obi-Wan over the edge of the platform. The Jedi fought to hold on to the side of the landing pad, defenseless against Grievous's blows.

Obi-Wan looked desperately around for anything that could help him—until he spotted Grievous's blaster! The Jedi reached out with the Force and drew the blaster into his hand. Without hesitating, he fired at Grievous, finally defeating the cyborg once and for all.

As Obi-Wan looked at the smoking blaster in his hand, he quickly tossed it aside.

"So uncivilized," he muttered.

Grievous was gone, and his droid army would soon be defeated, as well.

The Jedi were closer than ever to finally ending the Clone War.

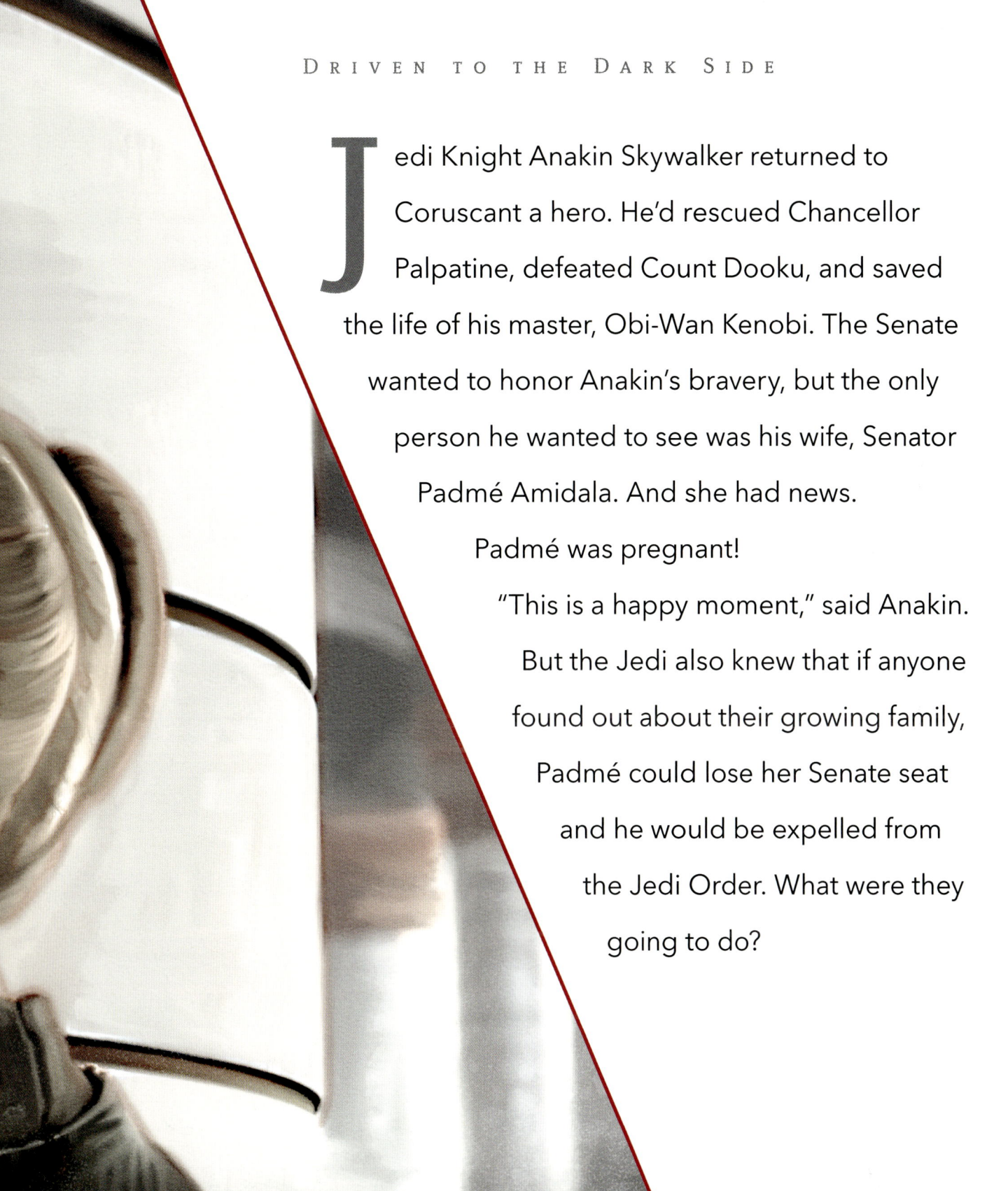

Driven to the Dark Side

Jedi Knight Anakin Skywalker returned to Coruscant a hero. He'd rescued Chancellor Palpatine, defeated Count Dooku, and saved the life of his master, Obi-Wan Kenobi. The Senate wanted to honor Anakin's bravery, but the only person he wanted to see was his wife, Senator Padmé Amidala. And she had news.

Padmé was pregnant!

"This is a happy moment," said Anakin. But the Jedi also knew that if anyone found out about their growing family, Padmé could lose her Senate seat and he would be expelled from the Jedi Order. What were they going to do?

That night, Anakin awoke from a frightening vision. He had dreamed that something terrible was going to happen to Padmé.

"What's bothering you?" Padmé asked.

When Anakin told Padmé what he'd seen, she told him not to worry.

"It was only a dream."

But Anakin swore to find a way to protect his wife. He wondered if Master Yoda could help him.

DRIVEN TO THE DARK SIDE

Anakin's questions worried the Jedi Master.

"Careful you must be when sensing the future, Anakin," Yoda warned. "Fear of loss is a path to the dark side. Train yourself to let go of everything you fear to lose."

Anakin stared at his hands. Padmé was his world. He would find a way to protect her . . . no matter what it cost him.

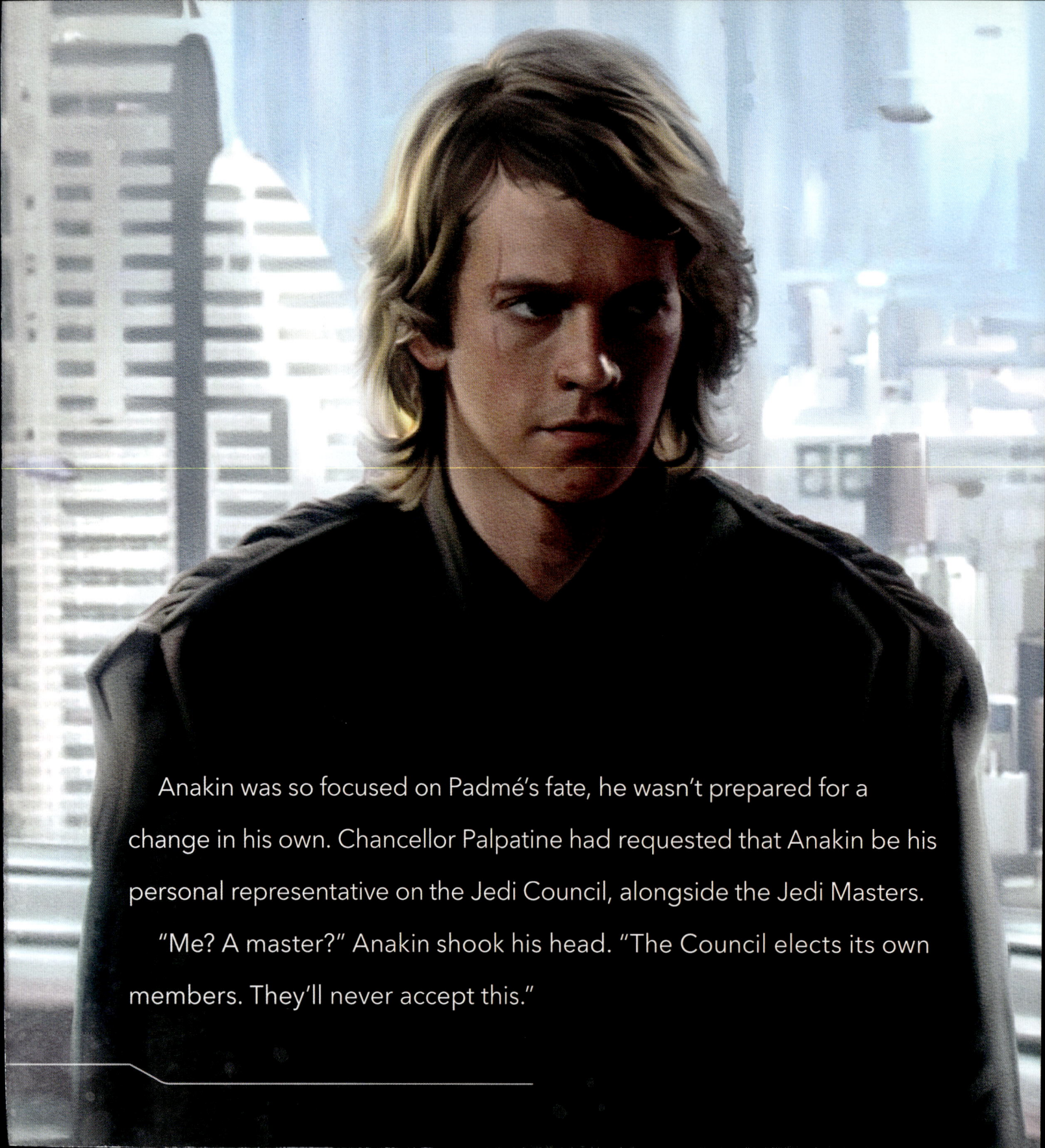

Anakin was so focused on Padmé's fate, he wasn't prepared for a change in his own. Chancellor Palpatine had requested that Anakin be his personal representative on the Jedi Council, alongside the Jedi Masters.

"Me? A master?" Anakin shook his head. "The Council elects its own members. They'll never accept this."

Anakin was right. The Jedi agreed to allow him onto the Council, but they would not grant him the rank of master.

Anakin was outraged. "How can you be on the Council and not be a master?"

Obi-Wan explained that Anakin's role on the Council would be to spy on Chancellor Palpatine. He warned Anakin that something about the Chancellor was out of place.

But Anakin trusted Palpatine, and he wasn't happy with his new assignment. The Council had asked him to act against the Jedi Code. Was this truly the Jedi way?

Driven to the Dark Side

One night at the opera, Palpatine told Anakin the story of a Sith Lord named Darth Plagueis. "He had such knowledge of the dark side, he could even keep the ones he cared about from dying."

Anakin sat up straighter. Could the dark side protect Padmé?

"The dark side of the Force is a pathway to many abilities," Palpatine confirmed, "some considered to be unnatural."

"Is it possible to learn this power?" Anakin asked.

Palpatine turned to face him. "Not from a Jedi."

Star Wars Storybook Collection

Darth Plagueis's story gave Anakin hope. He told Padmé he had found a way to protect her.

"I won't lose you," he swore.

"I'm not going to die, Ani," Padmé assured him. "I promise."

"No." Anakin leaned in closer. "*I* promise *you*."

Anakin was determined. But where would he find a Sith to teach him the dark side of the Force?

Anakin found his answer in an unexpected place. When he returned to Palpatine's chambers, the Chancellor offered to help him learn the subtleties of the Force.

"Learn to know the dark side," Palpatine said, "and you will be able to save your wife from certain death."

Anakin drew his lightsaber, the blue blade humming as the words fell into place. "You're the Sith Lord," he concluded. He vowed to turn Palpatine over to the Jedi Council.

"Know the power of the dark side," Palpatine urged. "The power to save Padmé."

Anakin hurried to find Mace Windu.

"Chancellor Palpatine is a Sith Lord," the young Jedi reported.

He wanted to help the Jedi arrest the Chancellor, but Mace Windu ordered Anakin to wait behind.

"Stay out of this affair," Mace Windu cautioned. "There is much fear that clouds your judgment."

Anakin was angry and deeply shaken. Although Palpatine was an enemy of the Republic, he had the power to save Padmé. And Anakin knew that he needed the Sith's help.

Anakin raced to the Senate building. Inside he saw that the Jedi team, powerful as it was, had been no match for the Sith Lord. Only Mace Windu and Palpatine remained.

Palpatine was using Force lightning to try to defeat Master Windu, but it was rapidly draining him of all his energy.

Palpatine called to Anakin, "I have the power to save the one you love."

Anakin paused. The Jedi had freed him from slavery and given him a future. But the Sith had the power to protect his family. He didn't know what to do.

"He is too dangerous to be left alive," Mace Windu threatened.

"He must live," Anakin begged. "I need him!"

As Mace Windu raised his weapon, Anakin panicked and used his own lightsaber to protect Palpatine. At that moment, the Chancellor sent a fresh wave of lightning at Mace Windu, forcing him out the window.

Palpatine rose to face Anakin. With his lined face and yellow eyes, the Chancellor's exterior form now matched the evil true self he had been hiding all along. He was the Sith Lord Darth Sidious!

Anakin was hurt and confused. He dropped to his knees.

"I will do whatever you ask. Just help me save Padmé's life," Anakin pleaded.

"The Force is strong with you," Darth Sidious observed. "Henceforth you shall be known as Darth Vader."

Darth Sidious had found his new apprentice, and the galaxy would never be the same.

EMPIRE ASCENDANT

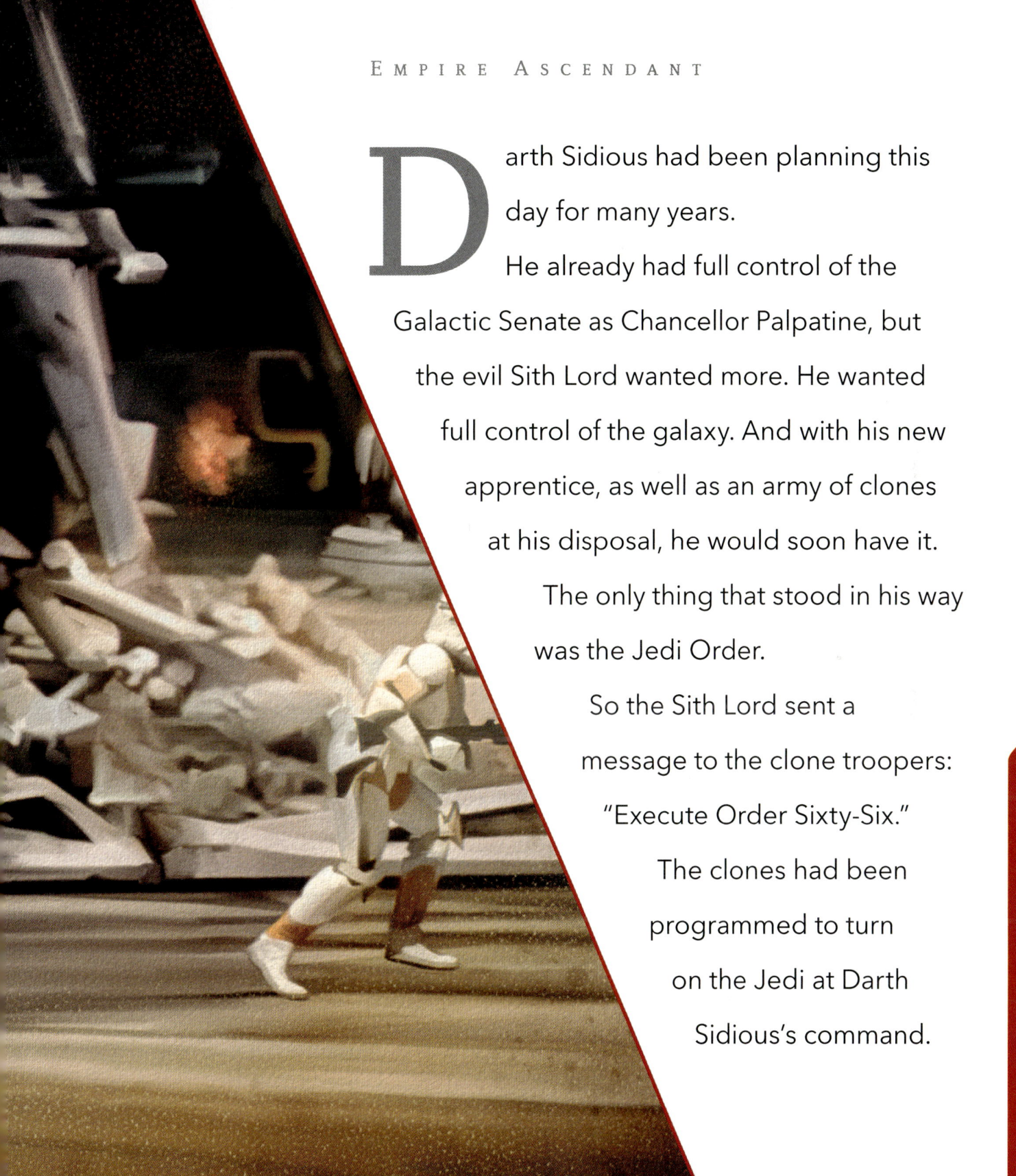

EMPIRE ASCENDANT

Darth Sidious had been planning this day for many years.

He already had full control of the Galactic Senate as Chancellor Palpatine, but the evil Sith Lord wanted more. He wanted full control of the galaxy. And with his new apprentice, as well as an army of clones at his disposal, he would soon have it.

The only thing that stood in his way was the Jedi Order.

So the Sith Lord sent a message to the clone troopers: "Execute Order Sixty-Six." The clones had been programmed to turn on the Jedi at Darth Sidious's command.

All over the galaxy, clone troopers turned on their Jedi allies.

But the clone troopers were not alone. After pledging his loyalty to Darth Sidious, Anakin Skywalker, now the Sith apprentice known as Darth Vader, marched to the Jedi Temple to destroy all he had once held sacred.

Across the stars, Master Yoda was with a tribe of Wookiees on their home planet of Kashyyyk, where he was negotiating an alliance with the fierce warriors. As the clone troopers' betrayal raged, Yoda suddenly felt a great disturbance in the Force. He felt the pain in his heart just before two clone troopers were about to attack him. But Yoda was not so easily defeated. Wookiee leaders Chewbacca and Tarfful helped Yoda escape. The wise old Jedi Master needed to stop whatever evil was already under way.

Yoda connected with Obi-Wan, who had managed to escape from the clone troopers on Utapau just in time. The two Jedi were joined by their last remaining ally, Senator Bail Organa from Alderaan. The three friends were quickly piecing together the day's terrible events. Obi-Wan asked how many Jedi had managed to survive.

With a heavy heart, Yoda told Obi-Wan, "Received a coded retreat message from the Jedi Temple, we have."

Organa added, "They've requested that all Jedi return to the temple. It says the war is over."

Obi-Wan realized that any remaining Jedi would head to the Jedi Temple and fall into the trap that had been set for them.

Yoda agreed. "Suggest dismantling the coded signal, do you?"

It was a dangerous mission, but the two Jedi knew they needed to protect any other remaining Jedi out in the galaxy.

So Yoda and Obi-Wan fought swiftly and decisively, defeating clone troopers and fighting their way through the halls of the Jedi Temple they had once called home.

Meanwhile, in the Imperial Senate, Darth Sidious gave an impassioned speech convincing the Senate that the Jedi had instigated the horror. "The Jedi attack on me has left me scarred and deformed." He raised his hands and announced, "To ensure security, the Republic will be reorganized into the first Galactic Empire!"

The Senate applauded. The new Emperor basked in his power.

But Padmé knew something wasn't quite right.

"So this is how liberty dies."

Once they had disabled the coded signal, Obi-Wan and Yoda stumbled on a hologram of Anakin's pledge of loyalty to Darth Sidious.

"It can't be," Obi-Wan lamented as he watched his friend kneel to evil incarnate.

"The boy you trained, gone he is," Yoda explained, "consumed by Darth Vader."

Obi-Wan had to find Anakin, but he did not know where his former Padawan could be. He hoped Padmé could help.

"He's in grave danger," Obi-Wan explained.

"From the Sith?" Padmé was confused and angry.

"From himself," Obi-Wan answered.

Whatever Anakin was going through, Padmé wouldn't let him face it alone. And she wouldn't help Obi-Wan find him. What if Obi-Wan were to hurt him?

EMPIRE ASCENDANT

Padmé knew that Palpatine had sent Anakin on a mission to Mustafar. She decided she would travel there by herself and save him. Obi-Wan expected as much. So when Padmé and her protocol droid, C-3PO, boarded a ship, the Jedi Master stowed away on board.

Star Wars Storybook Collection

Meanwhile, on Mustafar, Darth Vader's evil grew stronger. His friends may have thought they could still bring him back to the light, but if Padmé and Obi-Wan could have seen him in that moment, they would have understood. . . . The man they had once known as Anakin Skywalker was already lost to the dark side of the Force.

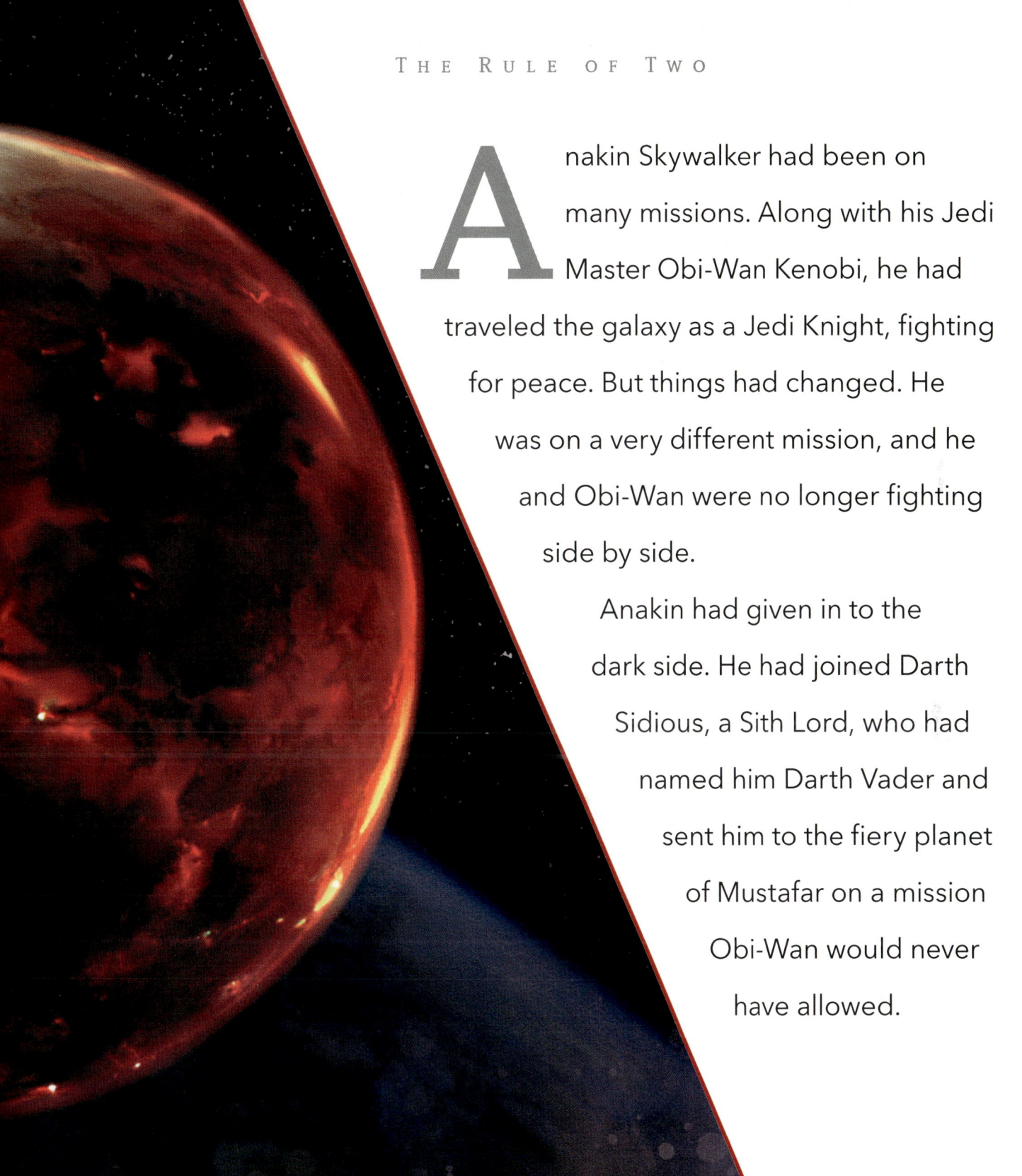

THE RULE OF TWO

Anakin Skywalker had been on many missions. Along with his Jedi Master Obi-Wan Kenobi, he had traveled the galaxy as a Jedi Knight, fighting for peace. But things had changed. He was on a very different mission, and he and Obi-Wan were no longer fighting side by side.

Anakin had given in to the dark side. He had joined Darth Sidious, a Sith Lord, who had named him Darth Vader and sent him to the fiery planet of Mustafar on a mission Obi-Wan would never have allowed.

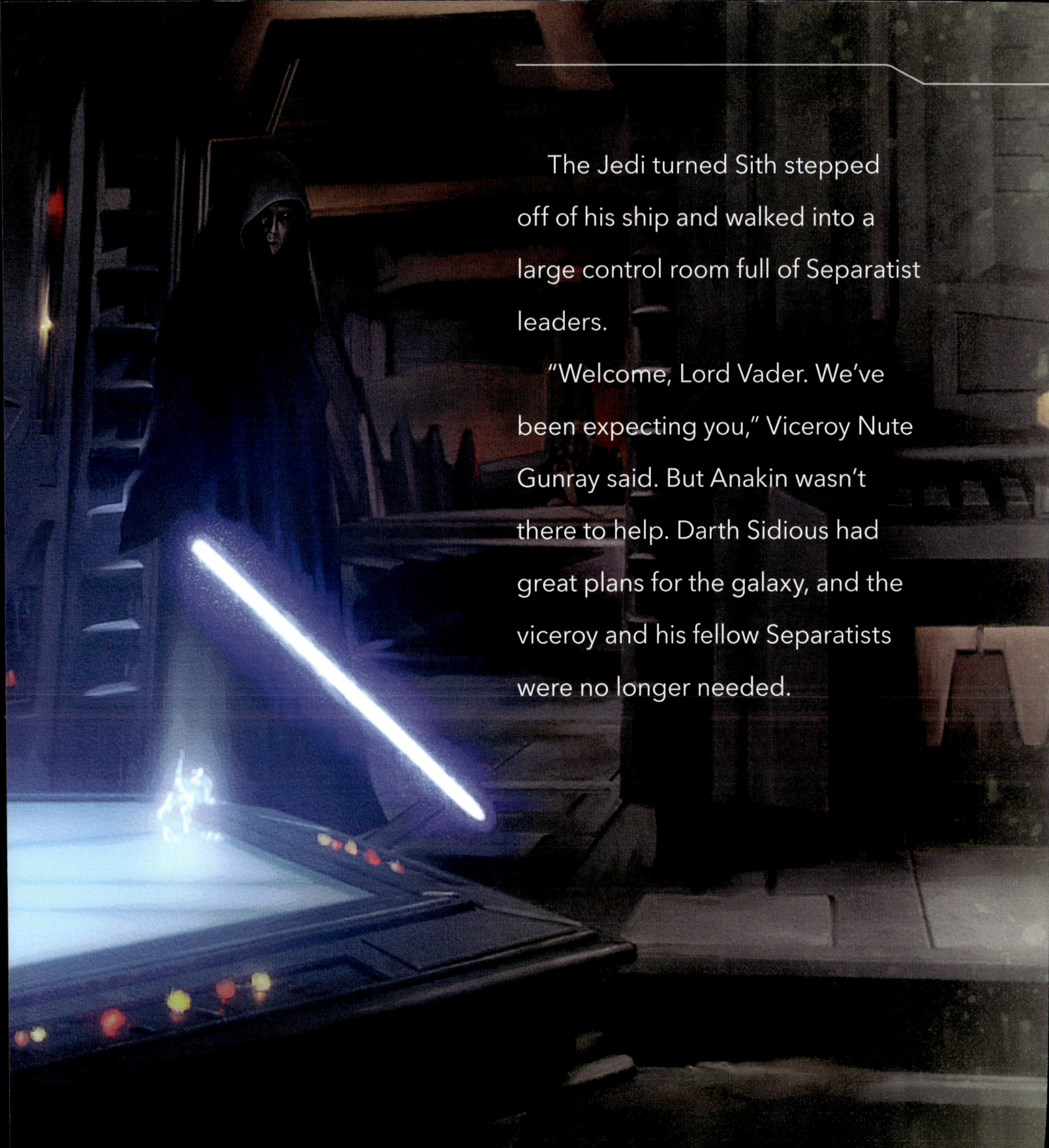

The Jedi turned Sith stepped off of his ship and walked into a large control room full of Separatist leaders.

"Welcome, Lord Vader. We've been expecting you," Viceroy Nute Gunray said. But Anakin wasn't there to help. Darth Sidious had great plans for the galaxy, and the viceroy and his fellow Separatists were no longer needed.

Once all the Separatist leaders were defeated, the young Sith contacted Darth Sidious to report his mission's success.

"It is finished then," said Darth Sidious. "You have restored peace and justice to the galaxy."

For years, Sidious had worked in secret, and his plans were nearly complete. The evil Sith Lord controlled the Senate, the clone army, and a powerful new apprentice. No one could stand in his way.

The man once called Anakin ended the transmission and glanced at a screen. A ship had entered the planet's orbit. On board was his wife, Padmé. She was supposed to be on Coruscant, waiting for their child to be born. What was she doing there?

Padmé ran off the ship and into her husband's arms.

"Obi-Wan told me terrible things. He said you've turned to the dark side," Padmé said.

"Obi-Wan is trying to turn you against me," the young Sith replied angrily. "I am becoming more powerful than any Jedi has ever dreamed of."

Padmé backed away from the man she used to trust so easily. He wasn't the boy she had met on Tatooine. He had become something else.

"Obi-Wan was right. You've changed," Padmé said, beginning to cry.

Just then, Obi-Wan appeared behind Padmé! He was on his own mission. Master Yoda had ordered Obi-Wan to track down his old Padawan and do whatever was necessary to stop him. Obi-Wan had stowed away on Padmé's ship, knowing she would eventually lead him to his former friend.

"You are with him! You brought him here!" the Sith apprentice accused Padmé. He used the Force to knock her to the ground.

Obi-Wan searched the young man's face, looking for a glimpse of the Jedi he had once known, searching for Anakin. But the young man had become so twisted by the dark side that there was nothing in him Obi-Wan recognized.

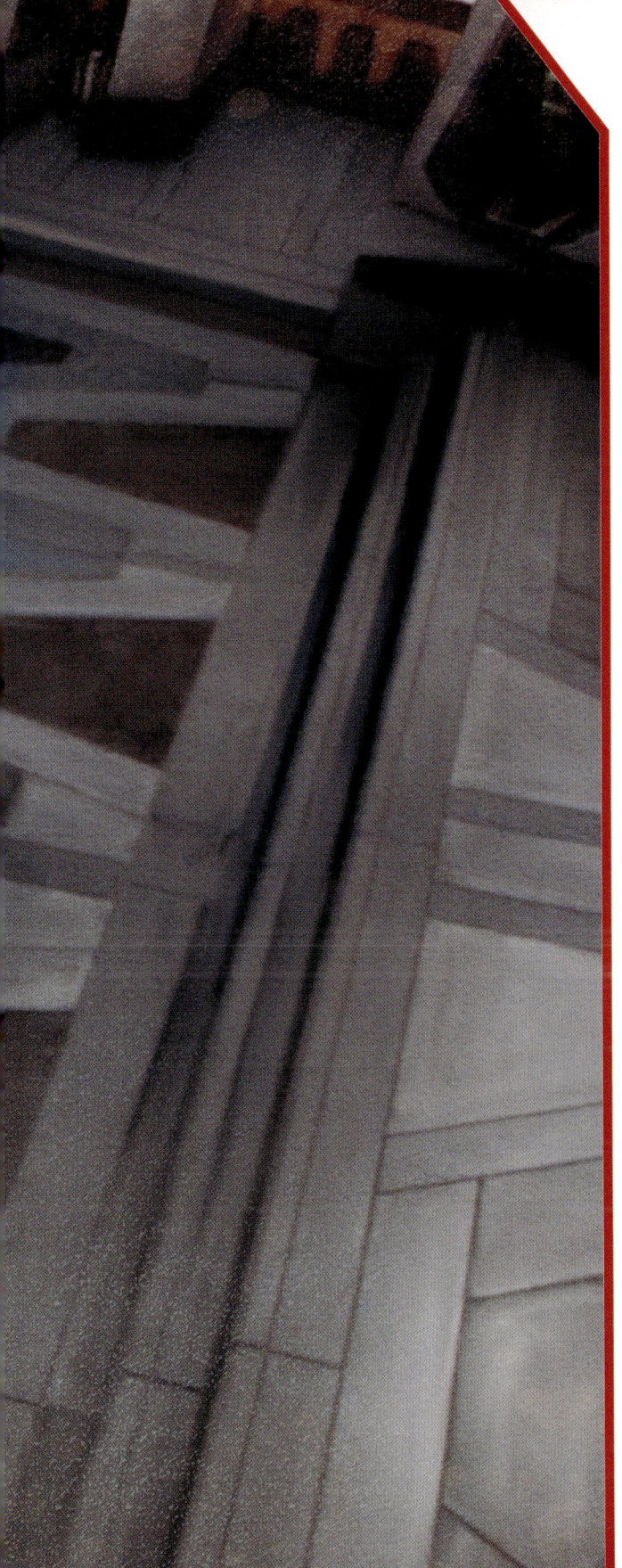

"You have allowed this dark lord to twist your mind until now you have become the very thing you swore to destroy," Obi-Wan told his former Padawan.

"If you are not with me, then you're my enemy," the young Sith replied.

"Only a Sith deals in absolutes. I will do what I must," Obi-Wan said, preparing to battle.

The young man leapt backward, lightsaber raised. Obi-Wan's own blade slashed through the air to meet it. Both blue lightsabers clashed wildly against each other as the Jedi and the Sith battled through the control room.

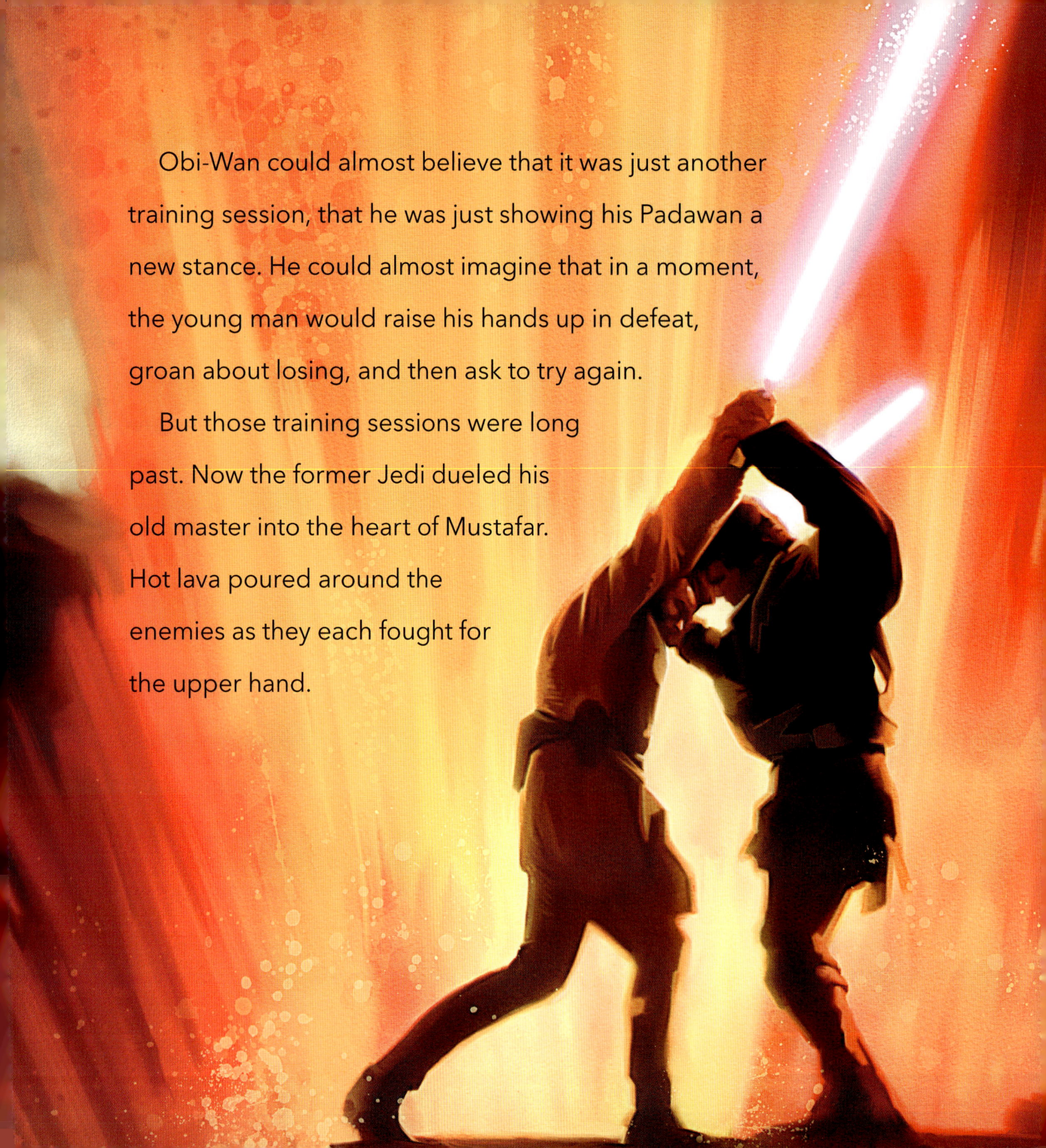

   Obi-Wan could almost believe that it was just another training session, that he was just showing his Padawan a new stance. He could almost imagine that in a moment, the young man would raise his hands up in defeat, groan about losing, and then ask to try again.

   But those training sessions were long past. Now the former Jedi dueled his old master into the heart of Mustafar. Hot lava poured around the enemies as they each fought for the upper hand.

Obi-Wan jumped to a small piece of metal in the sea of lava and stared at the young man he had once known so well. "I have failed you, Anakin," he cried.

"This is the end for you, my Master," the Sith apprentice replied, twirling his lightsaber and preparing for the final confrontation.

But Obi-Wan had taken a moment to look around him and realized there was a chance to end the battle. He leapt to higher ground, clinching the advantage he would need.

But the young Sith was so full of rage he couldn't stop. He leapt angrily toward his old master, and Obi-Wan had no choice. His lightsaber slashed, and Darth Vader fell to the ground before him.

"You were the chosen one! It was said that you would destroy the Sith, not join them. Bring balance to the Force, not leave it in darkness!"

Obi-Wan yelled, staring down at what remained of the boy he had once trained.

"You were my brother, Anakin. I loved you." Obi-Wan picked up Anakin Skywalker's lightsaber and turned away from the Sith apprentice.

Star Wars Storybook Collection

Obi-Wan hated all that had happened. When he returned to the ship, a heartbroken Padmé doubled over in pain. The Jedi Master needed to get her to safety.

As Obi-Wan piloted the ship away from the fiery planet, he thought about the young man named Anakin Skywalker and all the adventures they had shared.

DARTH VADER RISES

Darth Vader Rises

It was a dark day for the Jedi Order. With the help of his new apprentice, Darth Vader, the former Jedi Anakin Skywalker, Darth Sidious had seized control of the Galactic Republic, named himself Emperor, and destroyed the Jedi Order. The only Jedi left to protect the galaxy were Obi-Wan Kenobi and the old Jedi Master Yoda.

It was now Yoda's job to confront the Sith Lord.

"I hear a new apprentice you have, Emperor."

Palpatine was shocked to see that Yoda was still alive but reveled in the chance to be personally responsible for the old Jedi's end.

The two Force wielders raised their weapons and attacked each other relentlessly. They dueled out of the Emperor's chambers and onto the Senate floor.

Yoda jumped out of danger as the Emperor dismantled the Senate and threw heavy debris at him again and again. When Yoda finally managed to get out of the way, the Emperor attacked him with powerful Force lightning. It took all Yoda had in him to divert the energy.

Falling back onto the floor of the Senate, Yoda knew that he was defeated. If the Jedi Order had any hope of a future, he had to escape.

Crawling away beneath the floor, Master Yoda rendezvoused with Senator Bail Organa, one of the only friends he had left. Leaping into Bail's speeder, Yoda watched as the Senate building fell away behind him.

"Into exile I must go," said the Jedi. "Failed I have."

As Yoda and Bail Organa escaped, the Emperor hurried to the planet Mustafar. He sensed correctly that all was not right with his new apprentice. During an epic duel with his former Jedi Master, Obi-Wan, Anakin Skywalker, now Darth Vader, had been defeated and badly wounded.

Darth Vader was vital to the Emperor's future plans. Sidious commanded his troops to collect what remained of the young man from the fiery rocks and take him to the med bay on board his ship.

Meanwhile, hidden away in a corner of the galaxy, the Jedi tried to regroup. Obi-Wan, who had reunited with Yoda and Bail, watched helplessly as a heartbroken Padmé Amidala gave birth.

Padmé had secretly wed the young man once known as Anakin Skywalker.

But there was another surprise. Obi-Wan was handed not one child but two! They were twins.

Padmé looked at her children, and she named them Luke and Leia. Then she looked to Obi-Wan.

"There's good in him. I know," Padmé said, speaking of her husband as her eyes slowly closed.

Obi-Wan looked at the orphaned twins, knowing that they were the hope for the future that the Jedi needed to believe in—that *he* needed to believe in.

Obi-Wan, Master Yoda, and Bail Organa were not strong enough to take on the Emperor and Darth Vader. For now, all they could do was keep the twins safe from the Sith. Bail offered to adopt Leia and raise her on his home planet of Alderaan. Obi-Wan would take Luke to live with his distant family on the desert planet of Tatooine.

Yoda looked at Obi-Wan, sensing they would not see each other again for a long time. The exile of the Jedi had begun.

"Until the time is right, disappear we will," he said.

The Emperor's medical unit had done all they could for Darth Vader. To keep him alive, they placed him in protective black armor with a sculpted helmet that altered his voice.

His journey to the dark side complete, Darth Vader was more machine than man. Although he had failed to save Padmé, the man once known as Anakin Skywalker was too intoxicated by the power of the dark side to turn from it now.

The Emperor led Darth Vader to the ship's bridge. They looked out the window at a massive new space station that the Emperor was building, with the help of secret plans delivered from Geonosis by the late Count Dooku. With this Death Star, the Emperor and Darth Vader would rule the galaxy forever.

Far away from the Death Star, Bail Organa watched as his wife held their new daughter. There was a lot of work to be done. Bail was determined to create some sort of secret rebellion against the Emperor. But as he looked at his wife and daughter, Bail decided that his plans could wait—for just one day.

When Obi-Wan reached Tatooine, a young woman walked out of her home to meet him. It was Luke's aunt Beru. Obi-Wan handed the baby to his aunt and uncle and made his way deep into the desert. He would wait, protecting Luke from a distance.

As the twin suns set above them, Beru and Owen held their new child close. Little did they know that the baby was the galaxy's greatest hope.